"I DON'T KNOW YOU, JASON. . . ."

"Nonsense. What's to knowing someone? What you really mean is you don't trust me. Let's see if you have anything to fear."

Instantly, he engulfed her in his arms. She bent against him like a willowy reed bending into an irresistible sea breeze, and the protest that rose in her caught fast in her throat at the feeling of his hot breath on her cheek. Her arms were caught helplessly against his chest as his lips descended to claim hers in a passionate headlong dive into delight and desire. . . .

UNWILLING ENCHANTRESS

Lydia Gregory

A CANDLELIGHT ECSTASY ROMANCE ™

Published by
Dell Publishing Co., Inc.
1 Dag Hammarskjold Plaza
New York, New York 10017

ISBN: 0-440-19185-8

Printed in the United States of America
First printing—December 1982

To Our Readers:

We have been delighted with your enthusiastic response to Candlelight Ecstasy Romances™, and we thank you for the interest you have shown in this exciting series.

In the upcoming months we will continue to present the distinctive sensuous love stories you have come to expect only from Ecstasy. We look forward to bringing you many more books from your favorite authors and also the very finest work from new authors of contemporary romantic fiction.

As always, we are striving to present the unique, absorbing love stories that you enjoy most—books that are more than ordinary romance.

Your suggestions and comments are always welcome. Please write to us at the address below.

Sincerely,

The Editors
Candlelight Romances
1 Dag Hammarskjold Plaza
New York, New York 10017

CHAPTER ONE

The heady aroma of comfrey-leaf tea was mingled with scents of drying herbs that rose from the cellar. A light breeze ran in one door of the small greenhouse and out the other, carrying blended hints of thyme and sage and spices.

This was the best time of year. Springtime. Time to grow more herbs, time to be busy.

Judith leaned back and lifted the heavy cascade of nut-brown hair off her back, letting it fall behind the back of the chair. She put her bare feet up on the rail of the teahouse, an open wooden gazebo, and looked out over her cabin and greenhouse, her meadow and pasture. It was like something out of an Andrew Wyeth painting. And it was all hers.

Taking her last lazy sigh of the season, Judith raised a mug of tea to her rosy lips and thought how good it would feel to be busy again, after the lull of winter. In her cabin a pile of new orders waited to be filled—seeds, leaves, fresh herbs, potpourris, kits, essential oils, soaps—an endless, beautiful, busy list of customers requesting the fruits of her green thumb.

Then it happened again.

The cabin faded into a bright fog. The meadow became an apple-green frame around a pair of chestnut eyes, gleaming as though they had been burnished. A straight nose formed. Narrow strong lips in a trim jawline. The meadow changed to a frame of mahogany hair.

The face gazed into Judith's mind, a long engaging kind of gaze, as though he knew something he refused to tell her.

The mug clattered to the floor, spraying comfrey tea all over the wood. "Stop it!" she cried.

When the vision cleared, Judith was on her feet. She found herself staring into the printed browns of her muslin skirt. Her hair tumbled around her shoulders, casting shadows on her face. "Oh, how I hate you," she muttered to the receding vision.

"Jude . . . you okay?"

She looked up, almost warily. The meadow was a meadow again.

"Oh. Hi, Peter. Yes, I'm fine."

"You getting those things again?" The gangly fourteen-year-old boy launched himself from the ground to the rail of the teahouse and straddled it.

Judith rescued her tea mug and poured a fresh cup from a crockery teapot. "Yes, damn them. The visions aren't as frequent as they used to be, but they're still a bother and a half." She leaned back in her chair again, and Peter flattened his back against a post that supported the wooden canopy. "It was really neat when you knew my dad was going to get caught under the car way before it even happened. I never knew anybody who could tell the future before. Maybe you're a witch."

Judith held her breath in a spout of anger. Then she realized he was kidding, and sprayed him with a handful of sunflower seeds from the big bowl at her side. He laughed and batted a few seeds out of the air. "Now you're going to have sunflowers all over."

"And I'm going to make you shuck them."

"So what did you see this time?"

"That face again." Judith let her eyes lose their focus

8

in the steam of tea. She swallowed carefully. "I've been seeing that same face over and over ever since the accident."

"But it's been a long time."

"Almost eight months now. I don't understand it."

"It's easy." Peter struck a nonchalant pose. "Your car runs off the road, you end up in a coma, your mother breaks both legs, and when you wake up, you're psychic. It's like adding two and two."

"And coming up with ten," Judith added wryly. She felt her straight brow furrowing. Raising her feet to the rail again, she let the muslin ruffles of her skirt fall between her knees. "Whatever it is, I don't like it. I'm not a mystic and I don't go in for zodiacs or fortunetelling. In fact, I don't even know what my 'sign' is. Yet I keep getting pictures in my head. It wouldn't be so bad if they'd quit coming true."

Peter stretched his eyes wide and leaned forward. "Maybe Count Draaculah meet you in de night. Now you are desteened to be his slave. Mwah-ha-ha . . ."

"And Peter cleans the greenhouse before he gets beaned."

"Aw . . ."

"Hop to it, kid, that's what I pay you for." She stood up and he slid to the floor beside her. He was taller this year, she noticed. Last year he barely came to her shoulder. Now his skinny frame almost reached her height of five feet six. His shiny black hair and dark skin betrayed a Spanish heritage, but he was a cocksure all-American kid despite it. Together they walked down the plank steps of the teahouse. Peter stuck the end of a wooden spoon in his mouth and stroked an imaginary beard. "I have solved your problem, Miss Longfellow. Your body is telling you that it wants to be hugged by a sizable male of your species. You must date more often. No more monk imitations. I prescribe a love life."

9

"Enough, Dr. Fraud. My love life is none of your beeswax."

"Uh-huh." His young eyes bored through the pretense. "The last time you saw a man besides me or my dad was probably your doctor when you were in the hospital. And you were in a coma *then* too."

"What'd you mean 'too'?"

Unfortunately, Peter was right. Judith's life was isolated, self-oriented, tuned in to the wooded hills of Pennsylvania, where she concentrated on running her small business as a modest but quality-fussy herbalist. Her nearest neighbors were Peter's parents, the Viguera family, a healthy mile down a winding dirt road. The next nearest neighbor was another two miles beyond them, and that was the way Judith had come to prefer it. Until Peter mentioned it, she hadn't realized how long it had been since she'd thought about having a man around. *That's all I need,* she thought, *more men in my life.* She had lived alone in peaceful seclusion since she was twenty-three because, though she hadn't really admitted it before, men made her uncomfortable. Trust came hard or not at all after a long childhood and adolescence of watching her father cheat on her devoted mother, hearing him repent, profess his love and a long list of sorries, cheat again, repent again, in an endless cycle of pain and disregard for human feeling. Finally, Judith's father supposedly found the ideal woman and departed for good, leaving Judith and her mother to make it on their own.

Judith had made a sincere effort to overcome her bitterness. She had forced herself to go out on dates that she never enjoyed, always doubting the boy's reasons for asking her out in the first place, and she had fought to be fair with men as she grew into her early twenties. In fact, she had even been engaged.

And that had done it.

She had allowed herself to accept the passions of a

bouyant college man, a law student, during her short stay at a small college where she was trying to get interested in acquiring a degree in horticulture. She had allowed herself to forfeit her virginity as collateral for her future, and her dignity, quite wrongly, went with it. She had truly believed she had a chance to straighten the twisted path that had ruined her parents' marriage. Believed it, believed him . . .

. . . until she walked in on him and her roommate in the middle of a quiet November afternoon when she was supposed to be attending a chemistry lab.

Crushed by love and friendship in one fell blow, Judith had simply stopped trying.

She concentrated her energy where she knew it would do some good . . . on herself. She invested in her business, made it hard for the world to invade upon her privacy by moving out into the green meshed hills of the Allegheny mountain range, and built a life in appreciation of her own company.

There, she found satisfaction. It was a life-style where clothing grew older and out of style while gaining in comfort, and even the occasional twinges of loneliness and need seemed very much integral to the peace. She had love to give, but as long as she could remember, love had involved complication and invoked pain and drew up a contract too easily broken.

Luckily, her secluded homelife and business didn't allow for meeting many men, or getting out often. It had been years since she'd met a man worth dating.

A long time.

Except for "him." That face. No identity; just an incredibly appealing and captivating face. Why did he keep haunting her with those I-know-something-you-don't-know eyes? She sighed. Probably a pilot on a jet destined to crash headlong into her greenhouse.

"By the way," she said, forcing a change of thought, "have you seen that red vagabond of mine?"

"Yeah. He's in the meadow. He was giving Tribble a tour." Peter pierced the air with a shrill whistle, and was rewarded with a distant rustling in the high meadow greenery. A red face appeared, found them, and barrelled through the tall grass. The Irish setter plowed through the wild flowers, and as he came closer they could see the face of a small gray kitten protruding from the dog's mouth like a nabbed pheasant.

"Oh, my world for a camera," Judith mumbled.

The kitten eyed them as the distance closed, apparently enjoying the dog's full gallop.

"It's a trade-off," Peter said. "When I bring Tribble over here to play with Cashel, they exchange rides for chases."

Chases. Chases. Chases.

The word echoed in Judith's head.

Chase.

Her fingers raised to cover her eyes. Why did it ring in her mind? What was it about the sound that seemed familiar?

"What did you say?"

She blinked. Peter was looking at her. She hadn't realized that she had whispered the word, hoping to hone in on the meaning. "Oh . . . nothing."

Cashel cantered to a halt at Judith's side, allowing Peter to take the kitten from his mouth. All the while the dog's huge red plume tail was swatting Judith's legs.

"Ouch," she said. "If modern science could harness the power in that tail . . ."

"I don't think he realizes his own strength. Don't slobber on me, dog! Here." Peter took the spoon he was carrying and hurled it into the tall grass. Joyfully, Cashel ran it down and took out a mock vengeance on it.

"Peter! My spoon!"

"Sorry," he said. "I forgot."

"You *are* a rat. Forget yourself into the greenhouse and clean that floor. I'll pay you before you go home today."

Peter snuggled the fat furry kitten on his shoulder. "That's okay," he said. "I don't need it today. Next week is soon enough."

Judith narrowed her eyes and smiled knowingly. He already worked twice as hard as she paid him for. "You'll get paid today. My debts are my problem, not yours."

"Yeah, but what do I need money for? You can pay me next summer. Working around here's not really like working anyway, so what's the difference?"

"I thought you were saving money for college."

"College is a long way off. I'm fourteen. I'm an adult. You can't fool me anymore. I know what a creditor is. I see all the bills for your mom's therapy. *I'm* not dumb. *I'm* not ignorant. *I'm* not—"

"You're not subtle," she filled in, smirking gratefully at him. "Don't worry about me, Pete. I'm a survivor. I built a nice tidy business out of one itty-bitty pumpkin seed, and no creditors are going to take it away from me."

If only I felt as confident as I sound, Judith thought. Lately she dreaded the ringing of the telephone. Not long ago, she had relished the sound, for it meant customers making orders. Now, since the accident, customers' calls were interspersed with unwelcome demands from creditors. She hoped for a lucrative summer at The Calico Patch, but even a very good summer wouldn't support the business *and* pay off all those loans. Interest on the money alone was straining her income. What would it be like to have these debts hanging over her for years?

Her shoulders sagged at the thought. She felt the edges of her full lips drooping just slightly enough to bring a solemn worry to her face, turning sky-blue eyes a cloudy gray. She felt as though she were carrying all her financial worries in a bag over her shoulder as she stepped into the

13

cabin and turned to watch Peter and Cashel frolicking toward the greenhouse.

Was it getting that obvious that she was drowning in financial quicksand? Even Peter noticed. Judith realized her secluded life-style was making it easy for her to ignore her problems. Yet, she loved the quiet isolation of the wooded Allegheny foothills. Did she really miss men's company as much as Peter suggested? Were the visions of the handsome face actually what Peter joked about? Or were they more of her unwanted ability to know of future events? She hated the bizarre power. Telling the future was for Gypsies and economists to fuddle with. The doctors had been able to explain her coma, the concussion that caused it, but they hadn't been able to explain why she knew about the train wreck that flooded the hospital with injuries a good hour before the train was even in the area. She had begged them to call the authorities about the old trestle, but no one imagined this sick lady who had just come out of a coma would be foretelling a real disaster. Yet she insisted the train was heading for tragedy. Why had she felt so sure? Then, on top of everything else, it had happened! The train rounded the bend, hit the trestle, and *crunch*. Flying humanity littered the countryside.

And she had known!

No one was more surprised than Judith herself. What kind of a sorceress had she become? Just when she started to forget about the power, it would pop up again in some form or other. Like Peter's father getting pinned under that car. If Judith hadn't mentioned the danger, Sam Viguera would have tried to repair that transmission by himself instead of getting a friend to help. When the transmission came down on him, he might have been pinned there for hours. It was a good thing Sam was a superstitious man and took Judith seriously. No such luck for the people in the train wreck.

Now . . .

Now. Who was this face that had recurred in her mind since the accident? Was it a hint of another tragedy?

"I hope not," she breathed aloud. "I don't want to be a monster always predicting gory disasters." She went to the wall mirror, but got no answer from the blue eyes. A frame in a frame, that's what she saw. A wooden carved frame holding a frame of long wavy brown fluff that in turn cupped her square face with its high cheekbones and those lips that were one tad too full, colored with lip gloss she had made herself out of alkanet root, sesame oil, and beeswax. She touched her cheek. "Hm. Winter left me a dry face."

Face-ace-ace . . .

There was that sound again.

"Face," she tested. "Chase. . . ." She let the letters roll around inside her mouth, inside her mind . . . what did it mean? What was the heavy echo that accompanied those simple sounds? "I don't get it. Of course, Judith, talking to yourself isn't going to solve the mystery."

She urged the sides of her hair back with two tortoise-shell combs, tucked her feet into a pair of thongs, and slapped her way down into the cellar.

The cellar hadn't lost its winter chill yet, and Judith shivered as she gathered bunches of yarrow, sage, borage, and basil that had been hung up to dry. As she was bending over to retrieve a stray stalk of borage, she noticed an envelope, long forgotten, on the floor in the corner.

She turned it over quizzically and instantly remembered. The McNair Institute for Parapsychical Study. They wanted to pay her for allowing a psychic investigator to live with her for three months.

Turned them down flat, she had. Not a chance. No way. When hell freezes over. When rocks grow wings. When—

"When I really need the money. . . ." The words didn't taste so good. A stranger here, in her personal, private, sequestered garden?

15

She tested the images. Three whole months—a whole summer—not being able to do her housework without any clothes on. Having to get dressed before going to wash her face in the morning. Being "observed" for psychic events constantly. Submitting herself to ink blot tests and questions that seemed to fall off the sound track of a science fiction movie.

Still . . .

Ten thousand dollars.

She meandered back up the stairs, sat down, and curled her toes into the sheepskin rug.

Ten thousand dollars.

Oh, tempting, tempting.

Her hand drifted to the telephone. She heard the dialing, but hardly realized that she was doing it. The receiver was cool against her ear.

A female voice jogged her.

"Good morning . . . McNair Institute."

The unknown face filled Judith's mind again.

CHAPTER TWO

Well, she'd done it.

The McNair Institute was sending someone to live with her for the summer. At least they had the courtesy to send a female investigator. The whole prospect was so unappetizing that Judith had already forgotten the name they had given her. She had reacted like a woman hypnotized, as though she had just thrown out the window everything she had worked for to build the freedom and solitude she cherished.

Judith strode around her cabin the next morning in her birthday suit, relishing the brisk early-morning breeze from the open window. Cashel was exercising his best skill—sleeping—on the sheepskin rug, with the two cats, Mudfoot and Peaches, curled up beside him. Mudfoot and Peaches had raised him, and Cashel thought he was a cat. He hunted like a cat and ate like a cat, washed himself like a cat, and sometimes Judith swore she heard a meow from him.

She poured herself a cup of tea—orrisroot, this time—and slipped on a denim shirt to fend off the morning dampness, then squeezed into her best friend, a pair of jeans so faded they were almost white. They came up around her firm buttocks with kind familiarity, then zipped to cover her flat stomach. She had become pleased with her figure over the years, breasts large enough to jostle in a muslin peasant blouse, a waist kept trim by a vegetarian diet, and the blessing of long legs. And of course, hair that fell to the middle of her back. She had always considered her hair to be part of her figure. For a long time, through her teen years, her hair had been her best feature. But in her early twenties her figure had evened out, and her face had grown in to the large cheekbones and square jaw that had made so many classmates think she was haughty. How wrong they were. Under the tall, proud exterior was a basically shy girl, one who relished her own company and was most comfortable in her mother's kitchen dreaming scented dreams of a business of her own someday.

The business had happened. The Calico Patch was a self-supporting herbary, providing a nice income for Judith and a comfortable retirement for her mother, who lived in Pittsburgh, until the accident cost two months of business and piled them with unforeseen debts. If Peter hadn't kept the greenhouse going . . . well, everything would have been lost. If those plants hadn't been cared for, the heat kept going, the dome kept secure, there would have been no business to come back to. Yes, she certainly owed Peter more than his weekly wages.

There was a sound outside, and Peter's voice filtered through the door. "You up?"

"Yes, I'm up."

"You got clothes on?"

"Yes, I do. Come on in."

His youthful face squeezed through a crack in the door. "I smell tea. Do I also smell bagels 'n' eggs?"

"Only in your mind."

"My mind is boring. It's only a one-way brain. Not a satellite receiver like yours."

"How did you learn to get so cocky in only fourteen years?"

"Practice. Every night. By candlelight. Fries the eyes and strains the brain."

18

"You're a strain on the brain, all right. Get the eggs."

Peter took charge of the bagels while Judith beat the eggs and seasoned them with herbs. Oregano, parsley, thyme, chives, bay, sage, savory—the more, the better. It was a chef's horror, but somehow it all came together around shredded Monterey Jack cheese for a knockout omelette. She loved using her herbs, especially when she could break all the rules of convention and blend herbs and spices that no respectable chef would put together on the same table. *Guess I'm just a rebel,* she thought as she crushed bay leaves and peppercorns in her mortar and pestle. *I'm probably better off alone, no matter how good it might feel to have a man's arms around me.*

A cold shaft of regret ran up her spine.

She stopped moving and her large eyelids drifted shut. Fog swirled before her. She was unable to force her eyes open or her hands to move.

Eyes.

Chestnut eyes.

So close . . .

He stared into her mind's eye, grinning wisely, sweetly, perhaps too sweetly to trust, moving closer, eyes to eyes, lips to lips. . . .

"Jude?"

"Oh, Peter . . . I'm getting that face again. . . ."

"Wow . . . You want to sit down or something?"

Judith took a deep breath and willed her eyes open. "No. No, it's gone now." She shook her head. "Boy, is that spooky. It's like seeing through a magic mirror. Or somebody else's eyes altogether. Oh, Pete, why doesn't he go away and stay gone?"

Peter shrugged, uncomfortable with this kind of burden. "I dunno . . . Maybe it's another prediction."

"There's nothing to predict!" She beat the eggs furiously. "There's not even a full-length portrait. Not a scene to go on. No action at all. Just this"— amazing, sensuous, mouth-watering—"face!"

Obviously fascinated, but still uncomfortable with the idea of psychic visions, Peter rallied to change the subject, probably sensing that Judith was as uncomfortable with these occurrences as he was. "What have we got to do today?"

Judith forced herself to think business. "Uh . . . well . . . we have to fill several orders for culinary leaves and powders. Then you're going to grind the dry stalks while I make potpourri bags to send to the shops that ordered new supplies. After that, you're free."

His round black eyes danced. "You mean I don't have to clean plant trays today?"

"Nope. It can wait for the weekend when I can help you."

"Great!" He hated cleaning plant trays by himself. "You're a neat boss." He turned back to the warming bagels, and the perpetual rag that hung from the back pocket of his jeans came into view.

She had never seen Peter without a rag hanging out of the back pocket of his pants. Perhaps there was a rag sewn into the pocket of every pair he owned. Perhaps he bought them that way. Some people put their glasses on first thing in the morning. Some people wash their faces. Peter put a rag in his pocket. Life had its inevitabilities; this was one of them.

Judith was becoming painfully aware of life's inevitabilities. In fact, she was becoming a beacon for them. What was she going to do about herself? How could she live with these images of the future slapping her in the brain? They always seemed to come just when she started to forget about them, to think she might be normal again.

Why me? she wondered. *I'm nothing special. Why do I have to be saddled with this fortune-telling habit? Well, maybe something good will come of having a stranger—*

ugh!—living here. Maybe she'll find a way to stop these visions. Think positively, Jude. You've gotten yourself into this. Now you have to live with it.

"You ready for your omelette?" she asked half-heartedly.

"Yeah. No! If I go to the greenhouse and get some raisins out of the storage room, will you put them in the omelettes?"

"Sure. Fly."

"Flies in the buttermilk, shoo fly shoo . . ." Peter's voice faded under the scatter of his footsteps and Cashel's mad dash to follow him. Judith was beginning to think Peter was her good luck charm, rag and all. If it weren't for him, she really would be totally alone and secluded. She troweled the herbs into the beaten eggs, and sighed. She seemed to be doing a lot of sighing lately.

When she heard footsteps on the front path, she called, "Hurry it up, Buster Brown. The bagels are turning to rubber."

She got no answer. That was odd. Hadn't she heard something? "Peter?"

"Hello?"

It was a man's voice.

"Anyone home?"

"Yes, just a minute," Judith called. She turned down the flame under the bagels and set aside the beaten eggs. Another salesman, no doubt. Or worse . . . a collector. Someone to remind her that she had more debts than she could handle.

She pushed herself toward the door. "Yes, what can I do for—"

Chestnut eyes.

A straight wide mouth, lips parted in expectation.

Hair the color of bark on an oak tree.

The too-familiar eyes were like bullets boring into her skull. The familiar eyes of a complete stranger. A tuft of

21

the soft brown hair fell with childlike abandon across the straight forehead, over brows that swept like blades cutting into her mind.

He wore a business suit, but no tie, the collar of his shirt hanging open to reveal a long neck and a hint of dark brown chest hair.

Judith shook her head to clear the vision away.

But when she opened her eyes, he was still there.

"Hi," the image said, over Judith's thudding heart, "I'm Jace."

CHAPTER THREE

Jace.

Face, chase . . .

Jace.

Judith stared, helpless. There he was. Right there. *Him.*
Jace.

He stood a moment, being patient, watching her eyes
widen. She *was* lovely. Like a wild woodland creature.
Jason hadn't quite expected so appealing a sight. Most of
the so-called psychics he'd encountered were weirdos with
hyperactive imaginations, either dried-up women with no
gumption for reality or spaced-out students looking for a
new experience in the cosmic void.

No, this one was different. He hadn't really wanted to
tackle a three-month field study, but circumstances had
shoved him into it. If the hospital staff who treated this girl
hadn't encouraged investigation of her story, he wouldn't
have batted an eye in her direction, much less committed
three months to observing her.

But as he scanned the long waist, the jeans-covered legs,
the denim shirt taut across full breasts, and hair that
would lance Rapunzel with jealousy, Jason began to bask
in the idea of a summer with this barefoot nature goddess.
If only her brains matched her looks. . . .

After a moment, he nudged, "Jason McNair . . . from
the McNair Institute."

"You're not a woman!" she heard her voice rasp.

He put down his suitcase. "My God, you *are* psychic."

The insult slapped her back to reality. "They—they said they were sending a woman!"

"Didn't you get our call?"

"What call?"

"The call telling you that our lady investigator came down with a severe case of pregnancy. She just found out yesterday, so she decided the flight from Philadelphia wouldn't be a good idea. I needed a vacation, and I hate vacations, so I thought I'd kill two birds with one stone. May I come in?"

Judith hadn't realized she was blocking the door with her body. Him, him, him . . .

Jace, Jace, Jace.

"I'll invite you in," she said, jutting out her square jaw, "for tea. To wait until your flight back to Philadelphia."

"I'm not going back to Philadelphia. I'm staying here for three months. Excuse me."

The very force of his existence pushed her aside as he entered her cabin and looked around for a place to deposit his suitcase. He was athletic and well built, tall, she noticed, and quite graceful, evidence of confidence in himself.

For a moment, Judith was too startled to speak. Then she followed him.

"Look, you"—*you face in a cloud*—"I am not having some strange man living with me for three months. I have an impressionable Irish setter to consider, not to mention my own privacy. So please make other arrangements. Thank you, and good-bye."

That should have been that.

But it wasn't.

He turned to her—how did he get so close?—and spoke with a voice that could have melted butter. "You have nothing to worry about, Miss Longfellow. I'm a family man. Your privacy is safe in my hands. After all, it's not your body I'm interested in. It's your mind."

She opened her mouth to spit a retort, but her lips closed again. How could she get out of that one gracefully?

"Are we having breakfast?" he asked. "Wonderful. It was an early flight and I haven't eaten yet." He peeled off his suitcoat to reveal nicely shaped shoulders, broad and muscular, and rolled the sleeves of his shirt up to the middle of each forearm. Plucking the lid from the pan in which the bagels were warming merrily in butter, he leaned over and sniffed. "Looks good."

What eyes he had! Dark eyes, rimmed in Omar Sharif eyelashes, but without the heavy liquidity of ethnic eyes. Judith shook herself. "I don't remember inviting you to breakfast," she said rudely.

He straightened and hit her square between the eyes with a puzzled expression. "You mean I have to stay here for three months without eating?"

"That wouldn't be the case if you were staying, but you're not. I agreed to having a woman investigator living here. I don't even know you."

He breathed deeply. "Miss Longfellow, this is business. Perhaps living so far from civilization has clouded your ability to differentiate between business and pleasure, and although there would be great pleasure in what you're accusing me of, I told you once I'm a family man. I also fancy myself a gentleman. We're both adults, perfectly able to respect each other's privacy. Now, if you'll excuse me, I'll find the guest room." He plucked his suitcase from the floor and headed down the short corridor. On an afterthought he swung around. "Oh, by the way, you won't have to worry about feeding me. Above and beyond the ten thousand dollars, your grant allows for a monthly board allowance to buffer my rather boorish appetite." He flashed her a wry smile and continued his journey, leaving Judith to stare at the empty space he left behind.

Her lower lip curled in, and she was somehow pleased with the thought of his discovering that her "guest room" was a loft at the end of the hall, and that he would have to climb a ladder for the next three months.

Three months! He had done it! He had somehow bulldozed his way into her life and made it clear that he intended to stick out his commitment while forcing her to stick out hers. And for months her mind had been forewarning her of his arrival. But why?

Jace.

Jason.

Jason McNair. McNair. Like the institute! Was he in charge of it? The director, perhaps? If so, was he also psychic?

That possibility almost knocked her down. It hadn't occurred to her that a psychic investigator might be psychic . . . but why else would he be interested in this kind of thing?

Did he sense her feelings? Did he know what his presence did to her? Had he been getting visions of her face? He did stare at her for a long time before ramrodding his way into her life. . . .

In the middle of her thought, Peter and Cashel swirled in, a tangle of young limbs and appetite. How was she going to explain this to Peter?

"Pete, sit down for a sec, would you?"

"Whose car is that out there?"

"What?" Then she remembered: McNair said he had flown in from Philadelphia. The car must have been rented. "It belongs to an investigator from the McNair Institute for Parapsychical Study."

"Wow! You mean—"

"Yes. The investigator will be staying here for three months, studying these visions I've been getting."

"Wow . . . what's her name? Where is she?"

Judith paused. "How do you know it's a she?"

26

"How else? I eavesdropped while you were on the phone yesterday. A kid has to keep himself informed. You think anybody tells me anything? I learned early to find things out for myself."

"Well . . . things have changed a little."

"Huh?" He blinked. "How can things change in one day?"

Would I ever like to know! "The woman who was going to come—"

A voice interrupted them as though it had a right to be there. "Is breakfast on?"

Jason was standing at the mouth of the hallway, buttoning a casual brown cotton shirt whose collar remained open. He had changed into jeans, apparently taking his cue from Judith's attire. From his neck hung a gold chain with an eagle-shaped tiger-eye pendant resting in the hollow of his throat.

Peter's eyes shot wide and his mouth dropped open, then clamped shut. He seemed to sink inside his T-shirt, clearly intimidated by Jason's size and stature, not to mention the magnetic dominance in his air.

Jason McNair gave no slack as he moved to the stove and poured himself a cup of tea. "Hope you don't mind my making myself comfortable. I've never found much value in trite formalities, especially considering that we're going to be living together." He looked at Peter. "Who's your scrawny little friend here?" Lithely he moved toward them, radiating total control.

The shock in Peter's eyes was self-explanatory. He stood up and edged toward the door. "Um . . . I gotta go . . . I gotta help my dad clean the backyard . . . g'bye."

"Peter—" Judith ran to the door after him, but he dashed through the meadow at a ground-swallowing pace. Even Cashel sensed his panic and didn't follow.

Judith whirled on her heel. "How cruel can you be!

Don't you know how to be subtle? Fourteen-year-old boys are very sensitive!"

McNair leaned on the counter, crossed one ankle over the other, and sipped his tea. "I know. I've been there. Don't worry. He'll survive. A little taste of reality never hurt anybody."

"Maybe not from your god's-eye view, but down here on earth we consider people's feelings before we open our big mouths!" She stalked the room like a caged animal to gaze out the window to the meadow. "You shocked him. It wasn't the kind thing to do."

"It seems he has a crush on you."

She snapped a glare his way. "Maybe. But he's my friend first. He'll outgrow the crush, but a sense of betrayal doesn't fade lightly, Mr. McNair."

"Jason."

"What*ever*. I don't appreciate your audacity. You may live in my home temporarily, but my acquaintances are none of your affair to tamper with. I will not have you insinuating to people that we're living together."

He rewarded her tirade with a damnable shrug. The tea mug dangled lazily from his forefinger. "We are."

Her fists balled at her sides. "You know what I mean!"

"Certainly."

"I mean it."

"Certainly you do."

"And you go easy on Peter. He's used to being the only man around here, other than his father. He's been helping me since he was ten years old. I wouldn't hurt his feelings for the world."

"How about for ten thousand dollars?"

He succeeded in making her feel cheap with his insinuation, and she allowed herself a period of embarrassed silence. Tight-lipped, she moved to the stove to prepare an omelette that had been meant for Peter. "Sit down if you want breakfast."

"Are you going to say you're not out for the money?"

Judith kept her eyes on the omelettes. "No," she admitted. "I need the money. But I'm also hoping that the investigation will shed some light on why I'm getting these visions and how to get rid of them."

She heard the chair squeak on the hardwood floor as he settled himself at the table. "Well, well, well," he murmured.

"What?" Already she was suspicious.

"You're the first alleged psychic who wanted to get rid of the power."

"What do you mean 'alleged'?"

"Oh, come now, Miss Longfellow. We both understand the game. In all my years of investigating hundreds of claims, I can still count the genuine parapsychical experiences on one hand."

Bitterly she exhaled a puff of breath. "Well, add a toe next time you count! I'm not a liar." It took all her restraining ability to keep from slamming the omelettes into the sink and ordering him out of her house.

Jason leaned on his forearms and scanned her back muscles as they tensed in anger. He wasn't going to get anywhere this way. She was a fighter. The questions would have to come later, when she was more used to his presence, relaxed enough to give him honest answers. At least she wasn't a mental midget or a drifty bubble-head like the last two. At least he might look forward to some decent conversation. But first he would have to get her to relax.

When she turned to reach for the cheese and green peppers, he was standing inches from her. She collided with his firm chest, gasped, and backed away. Only his hand gently cupped around her elbow kept her near.

"May I call you Judy?"

"J-Judith," she corrected, trembling at his touch, his closeness. Her mind sent her flashes of undefinable colors. Was she getting a fever? Or was it the heat from the stove?

"Judith," Jason began again, "I want us to get along. Three months is a long time for me to feel unwelcome. I'd rather feel as though you might learn to like my company. Can we begin again, a little more calmly this time?"

Judith's trembling subsided as she lost herself in those dark umber eyes, and her anger ebbed away as surely as if it had been pushed. She hardly recognized her own voice.

"Yes . . . please. . . ."

"How old are you, Judith?"

"Twenty-six. Does it matter?"

"We like to organize these occurrences on various grids —age, sex, social status, background . . . that type of thing. Did your parents ever have any psychic experiences, or yourself before the accident?"

He was sitting at her table again, but it was now almost dark outside, and Judith was preparing avocado melts for dinner. The day had passed quietly, tensely, with Jason spending much time in the loft unpacking his clothes and organizing papers and tests that would be used during the three-month investigation. He also had spent time logging his first impressions of Judith. Knowing this, she was automatically defensive, resentful of his presence, and bitter about the cruel treatment of Peter. Peter did have a crush on her, but she was letting it ride out the time, as she had through all his other phases before and after he had started working for her. Jason's imposing presence had intimidated the poor boy, and McNair had played it for all it was worth. He wanted to be friends, but could she ever forgive him?

"No," she said, "to both questions." Suddenly she blurted, "Are you psychic?"

Looking up, he raised his eyebrows. "Why do you ask?"

She shrugged. "Your name. And why else would you be interested in psychic events?"

"One doesn't have to be a horse to be interested in polo, Judith," he purred. "But I see your point. My father, Leon McNair, actually founded and directs the center. My mother was psychic. He took great interest in her ability and has devoted his life to the study of parapsychology. As for myself, I have a degree in psychology and decided to join the institute a few years ago, to assist my father with his work. The institute is slowly forming a hypothesis that psychic ability is not inherited. In cases where it appears to be inherited, it was probably learned. We think children are especially capable of this power—reading minds, if you will—but they unlearn it by the time they're able to form complete sentences because most adults are negative toward ESP and telling of the future."

"So they're not the same," Judith finished for him. "But fortunetelling is silly." She placed a plate with the avocado melt before him. "The future isn't cast in stone. Any turn of events can change it. How could I have foreseen the wreckage of the train?"

Jason leaned back and closed a large hand around one of Judith's tall brass wine goblets. She caught a whiff of musk cologne as the air shifted heavily around him and was reminded of her mind's dogged predictions that he was coming into her life.

"I don't think you did," he said conclusively. "I believe you caught the mental pulsations of the people on the train, and something else told you the bridge was ready to collapse. You might have picked up on someone who saw the bridge, or even something as slight as an animal walking over it and feeling the instability."

"Animals are psychic?"

"It's becoming more and more accepted that they are."

Judith looked at Cashel, who was snoozing on his side on the sheepskin rug. Almost as if called, his lovely head snapped up to return her gaze.

"See?" Jason said. "I don't believe you actually saw the

future. I don't believe anyone can. I think you got a series of images, and your mind collated them, then projected the logical sequence of events and sent you pictures of what probably would happen if the events weren't altered. Like the computer that it is, the human brain assimilates and organizes the impressions that are fed into it. Your computer is simply working on a wide-scan pattern right now."

Judith slumped in her chair, her head dropping back slightly. "What a relief . . . that's a lot less spooky than seeing the future!"

He sipped his wine. "I'm glad you approve of my diagnosis. This whatever-it-is tastes very different. I like it."

"It," she explained, "is rye bread, mayonnaise, and avocado slices, heated and topped with cheese and alfalfa sprouts."

"May I express my undying respect. I can't wait to see what you do with a piece of meat."

"There's no meat in this household," she said, gearing up for it.

He looked up, and his attention chilled her spine. "No meat?"

"No," she said carefully. "I'm a vegetarian. Give or take an egg now and then, there hasn't been meat on my property since I set up shop here."

"No meat," he murmured, tasting the lack of his favorite food. "What do you feed your dog?"

"Dry dog food embellished with cheese and sauces."

"What are you going to feed me?"

"You're looking at it."

"Three months of vegetables?"

"Don't be childish," Judith said, pleased with having the upper hand. "I'm sure you won't go hungry once you see the variety of a vegetarian diet."

"You'll have to prove it to me."

"Glad to." She settled down before her own meal, and

watched him dubiously picking at his dinner, certainly not seeming to discover any ill effects in this new experience. He probably hadn't had a meal without meat since the peanut butter sandwiches of college years. "Where do we go from here?" she asked.

"Forward. I watch you and we record any extraordinary sensation you get, to determine whether you're for real or not."

She flared mentally. "You mean whether I'm lying or not."

Flatly he answered, "Yes."

She put down her fork and folded her hands in her lap.

After a pause, Jason leaned forward. "Now, you must admit that the train wreck is your only documented forecast. It might have been a fluke."

"I've had others. And I have witnesses."

"Amateurs. I don't take anyone's word but my own. You might very well be taking advantage of our offer."

"How dare you!"

"How dare I? Ten thousand dollars is a lot to risk on a one-time divination, don't you think? We need more than your say-so and those of your friends. If you turn out to be a fake, we keep our ten grand and you get the monthly stipend for your trouble. We'd go bankrupt if we didn't secure some credibility. We'd be suckered by con artists left and right. We might deal in the parapsychic, but we're a long way from plain crazy, you know."

Judith's voice was deathly calm. "Are you aware that you're insulting me horribly?"

"For that, I'm sorry. For telling you the rock-hard truth, I won't apologize. I've seen too many hoaxers who could make you believe they'd cornered the market on mantics. We've checked up on you, and know you could definitely benefit from a financial windfall. You're also somewhat offbeat."

"What is that supposed to mean?"

33

Jason smiled, almost wickedly. "Come on, Judith. You live in the woods, growing herbs for a living. I don't even see a television set in here."

"Hm," she huffed. "Maybe you are psychic after all. I don't own a TV. I listen to my stereo or I entertain myself in more constructive ways. I don't know what's so offbeat about that." She dug into her avocado melt with undue fury. Maybe she could get along without the ten thousand dollars.

No, she couldn't. But was it worth this abuse?

"I don't know why a genuine psychic has to have a particular life-style. How do you accomplish anything making such flaky prejudicial judgments?"

"Down, girl. I was just outlining the framework we're dealing within here. If I was judgmental, I do apologize. Your life-style is actually very appealing." Lucid brown eyes washed her body and held her tight in a gaze that might have been passionate . . . in another time, another place. . . . His mellow voice was skilled in calming, persuading; she knew that much already. Still, she allowed it to affect her in a way that was completely unsettling.

But she wasn't a fraud! She was having genuine experiences. How could she tell him that she had foreseen his coming, known his face intimately before they'd ever met? How could she tell him the sensations that had stirred deep within her at the coming of those visions?

There was a long heavy period of dead air. Crickets chirped outside. Cashel was snoring again. Or purring maybe. The cats prowled dark corners of the cabin.

"Please don't think I'm lying," Judith quietly requested, her voice like a blanket of despair, her eyes fixed on her plate.

His voice cut through her as coldly as a blade. "I'll have to reserve judgment on that. I've told you why." He settled back again and sipped his wine. "These are very

34

striking goblets. Now, why don't you tell me how frequent these so-called visions have been?"

Cool to the phrase "so-called," Judith forced herself to respond as emotionlessly as he had put his question. "Less frequent as time goes by. After I woke up from the coma, I was getting several a day. They've tapered down to a few per week. Some days I get several images. Other days, nothing at all."

"That makes sense." He raised one eyebrow professionally.

"How do you mean?"

"That makes me want to believe you. A fraud would be likely to have more and more frequent visions, or at least a consistency of them. This leads me to believe that the visions are truly connected to your head injury. It may have caused a portion of your brain to become hypersensitive. As time goes by, your lovely brain heals and the visions become less frequent, depending on the potency of the emotions involved."

Again she found herself hanging on his words. "You mean they'll go away altogether?"

"I believe so, as your injury repairs itself. Meanwhile we have an opportunity to sift out a pattern in injury-related clairvoyance. It's too bad you waited so long to take us up on our offer."

Was it only his words that made her feel so moved? Or was it his voice? Her mind had seen his face and longed for the sound of that voice. It was alluring, masculine and gentle, an oasis of security for her fears.

Could he tell her heart was beating against her ribs as he gazed at her so temptingly? Did he feel the same magnetism that clawed at her desires and dragged them trembling from their shells?

I don't want to feel this way, she mourned silently. *He's married . . . he said so. I can't be feeling this way! Please, heart, stop pounding.*

She pulled her sweater close over her breasts, hoping the silly gesture wasn't too conspicuous. The shirt she had on was substantial enough, yet she belted the sweater tight around her, trying to close in the pulsations of desire that came up unbidden from the depths of her being.

They finished dinner with a painful lack of conversation, with open lack of comfort—at least on Judith's part. Nothing fazed McNair, not even his propensity for insulting her, then mollifying her only to insult her all over again.

He settled in an overstuffed chair in a dim corner of the cabin and watched her. Oh, he was pretending to read a book, but he was really watching her. He would look away whenever she tried to catch him at it, but he definitely was following her with his eyes, like a lion hiding in a clutch of trees watching a juicy lamb and licking his chops.

She fussed around her kitchen under the blanket of his perusal, certain that the shaking of her hands was visible all the way across the room. She tried to busy herself washing the dishes and later studding oranges with whole cloves to make pomander balls. As she was using a sharp paring knife to pierce an orange with holes, she caught his gaze out of the corner of her eye and her hands lurched in a violent spasm. The knife missed the orange and speared her palm.

She cried out and jumped to her feet, knocking the chair away behind her. The knife and the orange clattered to the table, rattling the trayful of herbal fixings.

"What is it?" Jason asked, putting aside his book and coming across the room.

No! Don't come nearer! "N-Nothing. I missed, that's all. It's nothing, really," she babbled.

"Nonsense. You've hurt yourself. Let me see." His hand closed around hers, the warm skin making her fingers quiver. "My God. Your hands are like ice, Judith."

Oh, please don't be this close to me. "Please," she began, "I'm fine."

"No, you're not. You're nervous as hell."

Only then could she meet his eyes. "Why wouldn't I be!" Her tensions burst forward. "With you staring at me like I'm some kind of freak or sorceress or something! I feel like I should be hovering over a crystal ball or conjuring predictions out of a caldron!" She pushed past him and ran cool water over her injured hand. Tears welled in her eyes and flooded down her cheeks.

"Judith," Jason murmured, "I wasn't watching you. Not in the way you suggest, anyway. I was reading a book."

"You were watching me. I never felt so—"

Suddenly she stopped in mid-thought.

The water ran ceaselessly over her hand, but she no longer felt it. She was staring straight ahead, out the little window above the sink, past the kitchen witch that hung there, newly ominous.

All at once she whirled on him, spraying his belt with droplets of water. "You—you lied to me! You're not married! Your wife is dead!"

Jason's strong narrow lips parted thoughtfully, and she could see the tip of his tongue pressing against white teeth. For a moment she thought she saw a hint of—was it pain?—but then the professionalism slid back into place and he was cool again. "Very good," he said soothingly. "Perhaps I've judged you prematurely after all."

"Why did you lie to me?" she demanded, confused. "You told me you were a family man!"

"I never lied to you," he said evenly. "I am a family man. My family just isn't . . . quite complete, that's all."

"I'll say," she spat.

"Don't you want to hear me out?"

"I don't know what good it would do. You've cornered me into allowing you to live in my home and you mis-

37

represented yourself to do it. Do you expect me to believe what you say now?"

He took a calculating step toward her, by way of the sheepskin rug, not seeming to approach her directly. "Why not? I have to take your word for your psychic ability. But, Judith, has anything really changed? Are we any more or less attracted to each other than we were five minutes ago?"

It was an honest question, and she didn't know the answer. Was she frightened of him . . . or of herself? Of her own weaknesses now that there was no wife in the background to hold them apart?

"I don't know and I don't care to analyze it," she struck. "You may study my mind for three months—not a minute more—and you can bet it will be at arm's length."

"Judith, I only said what I said because I was baiting you. I wanted to see how strong your ability was to sense out reality by mental impulse."

"Or to put me off my guard!" The old distrust of men was snaking back, lurking in the shadows, ready to spring at her. In the back of her mind was a tiny voice telling her she was being unfair, but the snake struck before the voice could be heard. "You're welcome to my mind, Jason McNair, but my body is off limits!"

Her own horrible, unprovoked words echoed at her as she stalked down the corridor to her room and slammed the door between Jason and herself.

The only other change was the cease of gushing water as Jason squeezed the handle closed and returned to his book.

CHAPTER FOUR

He was near.

She was suffocating in the heavy aroma of his musk cologne. Then he was beside her, his thighs against hers, his warm body drawing impossibly close. His hand caressed her throat, trailing the subtle hill of her shoulder, cupping her breast and molding it to the shape of his palm.

"No . . ." she murmured as her body thrust against his like a separate being, out of her control. "No . . . please . . . this can't happen . . ."

His lips moved against her throat, tantalizing the soft underside of her chin with moist sweeps of his tongue.

"Darling," his voice rasped, "let me love you. I can't wait any longer." Caressing, probing fingers drew lances of desire from her body as she quivered against him. In her mind she knew she wanted the touch of his wholeness to continue forever.

"No . . . I can't," she cried, helpless, "I don't know you . . . you're not real. This can't be true. . . ." Yet she couldn't bottle a gasp of delight as his arm slid under her waist and crushed her breasts against his chest. His hands continued to roam, to taunt, to raise her to an exisquisite peak of passion she had never known before.

"No . . . no!"

"Judith . . ."

"No—"

"Judith, what is it?"

39

"What?"

"What's the matter?"

She struggled against his grip.

Then everything stopped.

"Judith . . . what's wrong?"

Her room was lit by the light from the hallway. She was lying on her bed. She shook her eyes clear of the vision.

Jason was standing beside her bed, silhouetted by the hall light, and he was grasping her arms firmly but carefully. He was bare to the waist, and his jeans had been zipped but not buttoned. He had obviously yanked them on in a hurry. The gold medallion swung lazily over her, and her eyes caught on it as it bounced alternately against the fine brown hairs on his chest as he bent over her.

"What's the matter?" he was asking. "Were you having a vision?"

"No!" She squirmed out of his grip and rolled off the other side of her bed. "It was just a dream. That's all . . . just a bad dream."

"Judith," he said, moving around the bed, reaching for her as though he knew she was on the verge of hysteria, "it's all right."

She mistook his concern for the terrible wonderful advances and backed against the wall. "Please leave me alone. I don't want you in my bedroom."

"Wait a minute, wait a minute . . ." His voice was as soothing as wine. "Take it easy. Are you sure it was a dream and not a psychic image?"

"It was a dream, I tell you!" It must have been a dream! She didn't dare tell him the truth—that she hadn't fallen asleep. Or had she? It couldn't have been a prediction . . . she wouldn't invite him to her bed . . . not now or ever!

"It was a bad dream," she said, forcing her words to sound calm. "I get them sometimes. It's gone now. I . . . don't even remember much about it."

"But the effects haven't gone away. You're sweating.

40

And trembling." Jason reached for her hands and managed to catch them though they fluttered like frightened birds to avoid his possession. "Let me fix you a cool drink. Can't you remember anything about the vision?"

"It was a *dream.*"

Jason gripped her arm with silky firmness, leaving her no choice but to let him lead her out of her room and down the short hall. The lights were out, and he reached for a lamp. "I was already asleep when I heard you. I didn't know if you were sick or having a vision or what, so I came down to check on you. I hope you don't regard it as an invasion of your privacy." His tone was mildly abrasive, just enough to scrape away her last defenses. He deposited her in the wicker chair next to the hammock that spanned one plant-heavy corner of the cabin, then started to pour her a glass of wine.

"I'd rather have milk," she said, fighting for some shred of control over the situation.

"Milk it is. You know," he began, "you never let me explain about my wife."

"You don't have to, really. I'm sorry you lost her," she said softly, lowering her eyes in empathy. Then she looked up. "But that doesn't excuse your deceiving me to get into my house." *And my life,* she added in the privacy of her mind.

He paused before putting the milk back in the refrigerator, and the muscles of his bare arms rippled with tension. She could see his eyes harden and turn darker, reminding her of the hard body in her vision. "Regardless, young lady, you're going to hear it. I'm not living here for three months having you think I'm some kind of gigolo. You're very lovely and alluring to me, but I've never dragged an unwilling woman into my bed." Tersely he added, "Or invited myself into hers."

Judith thought of her vision, hating the idea that the future was opening itself to her knowledge again, forcing

41

her to look into the tunnel of days ahead to know the—what had he called it?—the logical sequence of events. Him in her bed, making love to her! It couldn't be. It wouldn't be! She *would* find the element of change that would prevent such a future from coming true.

"My wife," he was saying, plainly forcing himself, "was eight months pregnant when she died. That was almost three years ago now. She was only twenty. I was twelve years older. I know that 'you're a lecher' look all too well. I got it when I married Lesley, I got it when she got pregnant, and I got it when she died. People always assume the worst of a man who marries a woman so much younger than he is." He poured himself a goblet of wine and slid one thigh onto the kitchen table.

"Jason . . ." Judith interrupted, "you don't have to tell me—"

He held up a hand. "Please. I want you to know." He took a deep breath. "I loved Lesley. As it was I had to wait until she was eighteen to marry her. Our marriage only lasted two years. The only thorn in our garden was that I constantly had to be proving to people that I loved her, making excuses for the age difference. When she died, I realized how little that mattered. She was my wife, about to bear my child. I swore I would never prove my love to anyone, ever again." Jason's voice took on a heavy cast, laden with disgust and resentment. "She died in a house fire while visiting a friend." He took a long drink of wine, lost in memories. "They told me it would have been a little girl."

Judith was unable to speak, and watched him in empathy, feeling completely foolish. Finally Jason tossed the remainder of his wine into the sink, spattering red droplets all over the counter. The goblet was next. He slapped it to the countertop with a sharp thump. "My family," he said, his words thick with bitterness and resentment of the social mores that had forced him to feel cheap for loving

42

a woman so much younger than himself. On the echo, he opened the door and stormed out into the night.

Silence settled in.

Judith felt awful.

She was frozen to the chair for long seconds after he left. A cacophony of feelings raged within her, from pity to pain to protectiveness and back down to indignation, then roller-coastering back again to realize how cruel she had been, jumping to conclusions of which she had become so certain.

She hadn't meant to be cruel. She was only protecting herself, her privacy, her own dignity. . . .

But was it worth her dignity to be as vicious as she must have seemed to Jason?

She had managed to convince him that her vision had been only a dream. A very bad, unwelcome dream. She had also convinced him that she had forgotten the details.

But I haven't forgotten. I remember everything. Every touch, every kiss, every surge of his body. I remember it all. And I hate myself for wanting more. . . .

CHAPTER FIVE

Judith stayed up and waited for him.

Not even her distrust of men or her desire to have Jason out of her home could make her cold to the genuine sting of pain in his voice when he spoke of his sad past. She knew too well what it was like to have love stripped away, to be helpless to alter the situation and be forced to watch one's dreams and hopes crumble at the feet of unforgiving chance. She couldn't allow Jason to walk into the cabin and be totally alone. No matter how unwelcome, he was still her guest.

And he was still a fellow human being. Judith stiffened her lip and remembered her vow not to let bitterness blind her to the feelings of others. In a wave of compassion, she poured two glasses of milk and made sandwiches in anticipation of Jason's return.

She imagined he was discovering the meadow path, introducing himself to the succulent springtime scents of the wild flowers that provided much of her livelihood, scents that would clear his head and calm his heart. He would walk past the rusty abandoned house trailer out there, avoid the muddy ditch, and probably get tangled in the web of barbed wire that once fenced off a cow pasture. He would detach himself from the barbs in time to see the moon resting exactly between the two nearest Allegheny mountains, as it did every spring at this time of night, and he would begin to regain control of his useless anger,

44

realizing, as Judith so often did, that the quickest reactions are usually the unfounded ones.

In the midst of her imagination, Judith saw not the meadow, but Jason's long strong legs as he walked; saw not the moon, but moonlight shimmering on his naked chest, drawing sinew and muscles of his arms in a pastel picture, highlighting the curves like washes in watercolor. She saw the firm, etched features of that too-familiar face as he regained control of himself and forced his memories back into place.

She shook herself.

"None of that," she muttered to the cheese she was slicing. Yet, why had she envisioned herself making love to Jason McNair? It had been only a dream—or had it? It was exactly like all the other visions she had had— visions that, without fail, had come to be.

"No, no, *no*," she insisted aloud, then glanced around self-consciously as the intensity of her voice caused the cats to hide and Cashel to jump to his feet. "Aw, Cash, it's okay." She put down the cheese knife as Cashel came to her and nosed her, asking to have his face rubbed. She turned and caressed his copper head, and pretty Irish setter eyes tried to comfort the distress he couldn't understand. "You are a big red baby, yes, you are, and I love your face, slobbery lips and all," Judith cooed, and planted a kiss on the velvety snout. He looked up at her cross-eyed and nudged for more.

"Will you do that to me if I grow a beard and bark?"

"Oh—" Judith straightened. Jason was just coming in the door. "Only if you chase the squirrels away from my greenhouse."

He smiled and drew the screen door closed. "I'll chase your squirrels any day. Are those sandwiches for us? What are they?"

"Tuna delight."

"Tuna? But you're a veggie," he countered.

45

"Right. The tuna is delighted because it's still swimming in the sea. This is a combination of greens and crushed almonds and other goodies."

"Delightful."

"I'm delighted."

"Your ladyship," he offered, holding her chair for her. He pulled out a chair for himself, but instead of sitting he tugged at the backs of his pant legs.

"What's wrong?"

"Oh, I got snagged in a patch of barbed wire and the rusty barbs broke off in my jeans."

Judith tried. She honestly tried. But her cheeks tightened and a giggle slipped out through her nose and before long her lips parted and she was laughing into her non-tuna sandwich.

"You jest at my discomfort?" he asked.

"I'm sorry," she said, still laughing, "but I was just thinking about . . ." No, she didn't want to imply that she had known what would happen. "I knew you were going to . . ." Nope, not that either. "Oh, sit down and eat your un-tuna. Here. Have some cheese. It's laced with port wine."

Arched brows lifted beneath a tousle of dark hair. "Do you do that yourself?"

"The cheese? I don't make it myself, but I do put the wine in, and no, I don't make my own wine. I'm not that provincial, despite the surroundings."

"So you knew I was going to war in the trenches, did you?"

"I beg your pardon?"

"That barbed wire."

"Oh, no, you can't saddle me with that one. That was pure coincidence."

"No, it wasn't," he corrected. "You knew there is only one path into the meadow that's obvious to a stranger at night. Your mind simply—"

"Projected the logical series of events, I know. And there's nothing psychic about that."

Jason leaned his elbows on the table and alternated bites of sandwich and cheese. His bare arms and shoulders were upstaged only by his muscular chest, tufted with a cluster of chestnut curls. He obviously was no stranger to a weight bench and a set of barbells. Thoughtfully, he said, "Don't you want to be psychic, Judith?"

"Want it? I hate it."

"Are you telling me that as a little girl you never wished you could turn into a witch or a fairy and do wonderful magic? As a teen-ager you never dreamed of dazzling your peers with feats of fortunetelling?"

Acridly she replied, "I was too preoccupied with the present to dream much of the future, much less telling it."

"Ouch. I hit a nerve."

Unwilling to give away her past, Judith sideswiped the issue. "I was a rather practical teen-ager. Very stoic. You know . . . somber."

"And now?"

"Now," she said, "I've learned what I really enjoy in life. I've built a world around myself that gives me pleasure and peace. I don't have much of a social life out here in the wilderness, but I was always awkward at parties anyway."

"Say, you know this isn't half bad." Jason scrutinized the concoction that stared back at him from between the slices of bread. "Different. I'd still like a slice of bologna. Or maybe a nice fat slab of chicken."

"You haven't even been on a vegetarian diet for one whole day and already you're having a flesh withdrawal," Judith accused.

"Crudely put, but true."

"Shame on you."

"You're right. I'll give it one more day."

"Tomorrow I'll introduce you to tofu and a few other

47

vegetarian delicacies. You haven't even put a dent in my menu yet."

"I've never fancied myself a quitter, so I'll give it a shot."

Judith smiled and stifled a yawn, took a drink of her milk and eyed Jason cautiously. He seemed to be enjoying the sandwich. At least, it was disappearing at a steady rate, and he wasn't sporting any grimaces of disgust to mar the statuesque facial features.

That face—it still unsettled her. Those eyes flecked with sparkles of bronze in the chestnut orbs. Yet, there was something hidden there that left her gasping when she gazed into them a moment too long, something that made her feel vulnerable, helpless. The level of *déjà vu* attached to Jason McNair's face, his eyes, his presence itself, was breathtaking.

His sitting there in nothing but a tight pair of jeans, and a ripple of bronze skin did nothing for her composure either, that was for sure. Was it embarrassment that made her feel this way? Had she been away from men so long that her womanhood had atrophied? Was she a teen-ager again, easily humiliated by a man's bare body?

"Would you be more comfortable if I wore a shirt?"

Judith inhaled sharply at his offer. Who was the psychic? Her, or him? "What?" she babbled, "no—not if you're comfortable . . . I-I wasn't . . ."

"I'll put on a shirt."

He exited, heading for the loft, and Judith gritted her teeth and threw her sandwich into the plate. "Damn, damn, damn!" she hissed. A trembling hand swept across her brow and found, to her horror, that her face was flushed, probably blotched with terrible evidence of Jason's effect on her.

He had done that deliberately! He could have just stayed quiet and let the whole thing pass, but instead he had chosen to call attention to his rugged body and to its effect on Judith. She had seen that in the quirk of his full lips and the sparkle in his eye as he bounced a knowing glance off her before exiting. Her long fingers rolled into a fist and she jabbed the edge of the table in mounting exasperation. He was toying with her! What a conceited—

"Is this better?"

He molded himself back into his chair. No, it was worse! He was wearing a summer shirt of thin cotton, pale yellow against his rosy complexion, with an open collar and short sleeves. The fabric stretched across his broad chest and crossed his ribs with creases.

"It's fine," Judith said thickly, trying to make her voice sound unstrained, "but you didn't have to bother. I'm a big girl." Her voice almost cracked and gave her away, but she managed to muffle it behind a chunk of New York cheddar.

"I'd never have known," he said calculatingly, "from the look on your face."

She slammed the cheese down and leaped to her feet. "You don't have any trouble keeping your footing on that pedestal, do you?"

"Are you denying that it's just a little exciting to have a man living with you? Especially after all those years of pseudovirginity?"

"How dare you!"

He stood up again and approached her. "No wonder the future upsets you so much, Judith. You can't handle the past or the present yet."

"Oh, can't I?"

He laughed, a short, infuriating laugh, folded his brawny arms and leaned back, half-sitting on the table, quite in control of the situation. "I really unnerve you by being here, don't I?"

Defensively she blurted, "Why wouldn't I be unnerved? It was quite clear that a woman investigator was to be coming here. I've managed to keep men out of my life after all these—" Her lips dangled open. She hadn't said that! She couldn't have said that!

Trying to cover her own indelicacy, she turned to him and backed away in the same movement, but as she inhaled to shoot some derisive word or other at him, she caught the mingling scents of day-faded after-shave and manly aromas so long unknown, now so enticing. Any sound that would have certainly sent him slinking away ended up frozen in her throat.

His hand escaped the frame of his body and crossed to catch hers. "You don't have to be embarrassed, Judith. You're a beautiful, captivating woman, and I'd be lying if I said you didn't have some effect on me. You have nothing to hide from a man who's willing to appreciate you."

Trembling, she whispered, "I don't know you, Jason . . ."

"Nonsense. What's to knowing someone? What you really mean is you don't trust me."

She quivered as he drew her noticeably closer. Her lips vibrated and her breathing was horribly ragged, sure to give away the sensations that plundered her body now.

"Let's see if you have anything to fear." Instantly he engulfed her in a firm embrace, his arms crossing her shoulderblades and lower back. She bent against him like a willowy reed bending into an irresistible sea breeze, and the protest that rose up in her caught fast in her throat at the feeling of his hot breath on her cheek. Her arms were caught helplessly against his rocky chest as his lips descended to claim hers before she could even capture the reality of the moment. Shots of electricity ran the length of her spine as his lips worked against hers, and his effort at proving a point became an excursion in unknown territory, a passionate headlong dive into delight and desire, drawing them both into the folds of a new fire. Neither had guessed it would happen, and even lost in the weakness of Jason's power, Judith was certain she could feel the same surprised arousal in him as his arms tightened around her and his lips moved hungrily on hers; she was sure he had never expected the heat that burst between them and flowered as it did for her. Why couldn't she back away, show him that he couldn't control her? What was this sensation that told her he was suddenly more sincere than he had planned to be? Had he planned to kiss her for so long, so captivatingly, with such prolonged craving? These thoughts were muddied in the wash of intensity with which his kiss devoured her common sense and left her mind and body as weak as a jellyfish riding a driving wave far at sea, senseless and completely at the mercy of its bearer.

Judith gasped as his lips released hers and he lifted his head to scan his handiwork, still holding her snugly against him as though sensing that her legs had lost all power to hold her weight.

The warmth that she had expected to see in his face was not to be found. His eyes were as cold as iron, with bits of cool copper glinting his conquest at her from within the chestnut orbs. An infinitesimal grin touched his lips, barely noticeable, but as thundering as a brass band as it showed her what he thought of himself, and of her.

"You see?" he murmured. "Nothing changes. Adults remain adult. The sky is still up there, and no one knows anything has passed between us. No enraged church groups clamoring at your door, demanding that you marry me out of common decency. Funny how the world has changed, isn't it? Two grown-ups can live together and be totally platonic despite the . . . rather obvious differences in physical configuration." He set her squarely on her feet, and ran his hand down her arm until it enwrapped her fingers, keeping the lingering moment in his power as he hovered there. "You thought you couldn't trust me, but now you know. You can. You may come to regret it," a wry smile moved his lips, "but you can."

Holding her with his eyes, he slipped past her and vanished into the dark narrow hall.

Judith closed her eyes to steady her reeling senses, unable to cool the molten core that bubbled and steamed within her. The only sounds were those of Jason climbing the creaking ladder to the loft, and the groan of arousal that escaped from her own lips.

CHAPTER SIX

Through the next couple of days Judith somehow forced herself to keep to her daily regimen of early rising and a stretching session, but it all had to be done in the confines of her bedroom. She couldn't even brush her teeth or have a cup of Chinese breakfast tea before she was completely dressed, and this annoyed her and made her more aware of the intrusion in her life. Jason had taken the upper hand; he knew she had no choice but to let him stay if she was to dig herself out of her financial troubles.

Jason had been preoccupied most of the time, arranging tests and articles that pertained to her, and Judith had managed to keep to her duties in the greenhouse, although she found herself more and more drawn by Jason's captivating presence. She hated the attraction he aroused in her, despised herself for her weakness when she found excuses to go into the cabin where he was reading, for reasons she could not even explain to herself.

It worried her that she had seen so little of Peter since Jason's arrival. She hoped his feelings weren't hurt too badly, but she forced herself not to phone the Viguera house to talk to him. She didn't want to mar his dignity any more than it had already been marred. Young boys were little different from men in that; they held their pride above anything that should be more meaningful.

On a particularly bright morning, Judith crawled out of bed and yanked on a simple blue T-shirt that was intimate-

53

ly snug and had a rounded neckline, lower than most T-shirts. Musing over her wardrobe, she realized she hadn't bought anything new or modern for herself in what actually amounted to years. Her luxurious hair wasn't long and untrimmed for any country effect; it was because she had become too (was it lazy?) self-indulgent to bother having it styled, or too (yes, it was lazy) busy to take time to set and dry it when she rarely went anywhere to show it off. Fortunately, there was so much naturally wavy bulk to it that it looked much better than she thought it did. Although when set and curled her waist-length locks were indeed gorgeous, they seemed to complement her features and her life-style even better when allowed to go their own way. This morning, however, in blatant rebellion, she took ten minutes to weave the two strands that usually fell forward over her shoulders into braids on each side. Though she heard Jason rising, dressing, and padding about her kitchen, she deliberately refused to hurry. In fact, she purposefully took her time, and made sure to bang the closet door shut, clap closed a couple of dresser drawers, and drop her brush at least once so that he would *know* she was in no rush to subject herself to his company.

The sounds of Jason's presence had an unexpected effect on her. Had it been so long?

They reminded her of the tension in her childhood home—sounds of her father rising in the morning after spending half the night in another woman's bed. The buzz of the shaver, the flats of palms slapping after-shave on pinkened cheeks, the tread of a man's heavy footsteps. The recollection of awakening to those sounds as a frightened child and as a bitter teen-ager sliced through her with infinitely more potency than she would have guessed they might.

So the memories had not faded after all. Perhaps they never would.

After a while the noise from the bathroom and kitchen

54

stopped, and she assumed he had settled down to read or had stepped outside to enjoy the sweet-smelling meadow morning. She wished suddenly that she was out there herself.

Determined not to miss the perfect privacy of her morning, Judith stepped to the window, parted the curtains, and lifted the window all the way open, then raised the screen.

Wild flower scents rushed in at her, freshly released by the drying dew, and she automatically identified roses, toadflax, summer savory, lilac.

Oh, how she wished she was alone! Her precious solitude was lost to her need for money. She knew she was luckier than most people who found themselves in unexpected debt, and that Jason's presence would ultimately allow her to keep her business, but why, oh, why couldn't they have found another woman to send? Men caused such damned complications!

Her thoughts were cut short by the sudden gunning of a car engine. She tugged at the rusted screen until it shut, and hurried out of her bedroom in time to catch a glimpse of the rented silver Datsun vanishing down the road in a gust of dirt.

"Now, where's he going?" she wondered. Shaking her head, she hastily added, "Oh, just be glad he's going." But she remained at the screen door for many moments, unable to break away.

Judith took advantage of Jason's absence to get her day's plans in order and to start a job that would keep her occupied long after his return and provide excuses for her to be out of the cabin. She chose a task that would look so boring that he wouldn't offer to help: transplanting indoor seedlings into a half barrel of soil.

The greenhouse was an especially cheery place. Herbs grew everywhere—plant trays filled with tender seedlings and huge half barrels crammed with mature plants made an oasis of greenery all year-round. Once the evenings warmed up and the last traces of chilly dampness and any chance of frost went away for the season, she would plant a huge outdoor garden of sun-loving herbs and spices. Until then, though, as she had all winter, she had to tend indoor plants and rely upon them to fill her orders. All along one wall of the greenhouse were tiny annual herblings that would eventually go outside to join the perennials that would come up on their own. Other herbs, like the sensitive tropical kavakava and the desert-born frankincense, stayed in the greenhouse all the time, thriving in the moist, regulated atmosphere. Later in the summer, Judith would dredge out the autumn muck from her pond and plant a water garden of lotus, water chestnuts, watercress, and sweet flag. The whole idea was enrapturing! Oh, how she loved her work!

She was elbow-deep in black soil and Michigan peat moss encouraging tiny rootballs into the big half barrel when she heard Cashel's "happy" bark and peered through the greenhouse glass to see what was going on. A trickle of perspiration streamed from her throat to the delicate cavern of her breasts, held loosely as they were in a skimpy terry cloth camisole that she used while working in the greenhouse. She also wore a pair of sunglasses to allay the brightness of the sun flooding in from all sides and beating down through the glass roof. She couldn't see anything, and, assuming Cashel was after a chipmunk, she went back to her tedious work of loosening and spreading each rootball and filling the holes with peat moss, leaving enough room for each seedling to grow to luxurious maturity.

Then she heard footsteps and looked for a bare spot in the tall variegated foliage that burgeoned all around her.

"Only me," a voice admitted, and Peter appeared between a huge potted fig and a trellis of old damask roses.

Judith let her gloved hands rest on the edge of the barrel. "Peter," she said softly. "I've missed you."

He shrugged his bony shoulders. "I got a job to do."

She smiled. "That's my guy. I knew you wouldn't let me down."

"Heck, no," he said, and made his way familiarly through the rows of plant trays and strawberry pots. "Just because you have a pet gorilla doesn't mean I'm going to shirk my duties." He began crumbling old soil from the taproot of a seedling.

Trying not to laugh, Judith asked, "Aren't you the one who said I should have more men in my life?"

He shrugged again. "Yeah, but I thought you were gonna wait for me."

"You think I'd make you a good wife?"

"Yeah, but I don't want any kids."

"You don't? Why not?"

"Kids are a pain."

"How do you know, Pete?"

"Simple. I'm a kid," he said, "and I'm a pain."

This time she caught the quirkish grin he was trying to hide and laughed heartily. "You sure are! Besides, I want kids someday."

He looked up and all shame faded. "For real? Then I guess you can't wait for me."

Suspicious, she narrowed her eyes. "And why not?"

"Cuz," he began, "by then you'll be senile."

He dashed behind a tier of mature herbs in time to miss getting a clump of soil in the ear.

By the time Jason returned, Peter and Judith had finished transplanting the seedlings and were hard at work shucking last year's sunflower heads for this year's patch and separating last year's good pumpkin seeds from the bad ones for the same reasons. Judith was apprehensive, keen to what would be Peter's reaction to Jason, and to Jason's obviously deliberate lack of sensitivity to the boy.

But just as she had to learn to tolerate McNair's presence, so Peter would have to also. The whole idea of Peter's having to dread coming to her place was almost as loathsome to Judith as having her privacy so blatantly disrupted. She owed a lot to Peter, in a way as much as she owed her creditors. Maybe more. Tension made her arms shiver when she saw Jason approaching from the cabin.

"Good morning, Judith," he said with melodic self-confidence. "Don't vegetarians eat breakfast?"

She bristled at his impudence. "I find it healthier to wait awhile before eating. I eat less, and I'm more selective about what I eat."

Jason smirked. Was he put off by her careful avoidance of offering to make him breakfast? He was welcome to get his own, but Judith decided obstinately that it would be in her favor to make him realize he wasn't going to distract her from her business obligations.

She was tensely awaiting his reaction when Peter came up from the greenhouse storage cellar, and Judith held her breath and forced herself to keep working.

Peter paused a moment, but the weight of the sack of peat he was carrying forced him to finish his trek into the middle area of the greenhouse, near the workbench where Judith was, not far from the door where Jason stood observing them with aplomb.

"Hi," Jason ventured.

"Hi." Peter's response was still laced with timidity. Jason, of course, looked imposing and masculine in tight jeans and a V-necked shirt of a tempting shade of celery green.

"You're Peter, aren't you?" It was the only concession he would give the boy. He darn well knew it was Peter.

"Yeah, I guess," Peter grunted, trying to act too busy to talk to him.

Judith tried to think of some way to ease the situation, but all possibilities seemed too awkward.

58

"My name's Jace. I understand this place would fall apart without you."

Peter slowed his feverish pace of layering the plant trays with soil and peat, and Judith noticed he actually stood up straighter and met Jason's gaze. "Yeah, I guess it would," he said.

Judith, speechless, gave Jason a grateful smile when Peter wasn't looking.

"Maybe you can teach me a few things so I won't be so superfluous during the next few months." It was all concession. Judith knew it. She could only hope that Peter didn't, that he wouldn't feel patronized.

"Maybe," Peter said tersely. There was a note of "probably not" in his tone, however, and Judith sensed that the boy wanted to keep any upper hand he could get.

"Where did you go this morning?" she interrupted, trying to pace out the conversation and turn its tide.

"I drove into town to pick up a shipment of personal belongings and reference books. When I left the institute so hurriedly, I had my assistant collect them with instructions to fly them out to me. Since I didn't know precisely where you lived, I had them sent to the local postal service by general delivery. Do you know I actually passed a place called Shoe Corners?"

"I know it well."

"I daresay it has a history."

"It might. I don't know."

"I'd love to find out. How does a place get a name like Shoe Corners?"

Surprisingly enough, Peter spoke up. That was the secret, of course; mention history and Peter's tongue would never stop wagging. "It was a trapper who came from Austria in 1802 and trapped in these mountains," he explained. "He got caught in one of his own traps one night and drowned in the river. His name was Shuess."

Jason threw back his head and laughed, white teeth

59

glittering in the brightness of the greenhouse. "That's quite a story." He leaned one elbow on the utility sink and cocked his hip gracefully.

"You're . . . interested in history?" Peter asked dubiously.

Jason folded his arms as though in contemplation. The green shirt molded tight folds from his trim waist to his muscular chest, and the short sleeve strained around rock-hard muscles in his arms. "Between you, me, and the Spanish Armada," he droned, "I'm more than a tad fond of the scholarly perusal of times past."

Glibly Judith interrupted, "Right, but do you like history?"

She got a comradely giggle out of Peter.

Well, at least they have something in common, she thought, with mild relief. She didn't really care how Jason treated her, callously or with snide amusement, as long as he treated Peter with some respect. Jason commanded an easygoing sophistication and elicited responses from Judith that she couldn't explain, but Peter had earned an honored place at The Calico Patch with loyalty, diligence, and plain hard work. Whatever effect Jason McNair had on her, she wouldn't allow him to hurt Peter.

"You like history too, do you, Peter?"

"Yeah, kinda."

"What parts of history?"

Another adolescent shrug. "Ancient stuff. Wars. Pioneers."

"Oh? Who's your favorite character from history?"

Peter turned more toward him, his interests overcoming the intimidation of Jason's brawny good looks. "Alexander, I guess."

"Ah, of course. Alexander the Great. Did you know his father's grave was discovered in Vergina, Greece?"

"Yeah!" Peter's eyes lit up like light bulbs. "Do you agree it was Phillip's grave?"

"Certainly. The greaves and the second sarcophagus did it for me."

Peter almost dropped the plant tray. "Me too! And the little heads of Alexander and his parents!"

"And the sheer magnitude of wealth in the grave."

"Yeah! It couldn't be anybody less than a king!"

"Yoo-hoo," Judith said slowly. "Remember me? Tell me what you're talking about."

"And the thing that went around his head . . . the . . . the . . ."

"The diadem," Jason finished. "I don't see how anyone could mistake the grave for anyone's but that of Phillip the Second of Macedon. Phillip was the only king to die in that period."

"I got a great book about it at home!" Peter blathered. "Wanna come over to my house and look? I got lots of stuff!"

"Of course. You don't mind, do you, Judith?" It was *not* a request. "Lead on, Peter."

"Mind? Why should I mind?" Judith answered, puzzled by the sudden change in current. Hadn't she been paddling in a completely different river a moment ago?

"Who do you think assassinated Phillip?" Peter inquired.

"Pausanius, of course."

"Yeah, but who do you think planned it? Do you think Alexander did it?"

"Not a chance. He respected fair play and admired his father too much to have had anything to do with it."

"That's what I think!"

"So who engineered it?"

"Olympias! His mother!"

"Good man. My conclusions exactly."

Jason was heading out the door, with Peter dancing at his side, caught up in the mutual interest they had discovered.

61

Judith remained at the sink, elbow deep in soil, her lips parted in astonishment, unable to speak—to get a word in edgewise—as Jason and Peter ignored her thoroughly and headed for Jason's car.

"What about me?" she questioned softly, but only the herbs heard her. "Isn't anybody going to ask me to go along?" Only the muffled gunning of the engine answered her.

Her voice faded pathetically, and she couldn't understand why her revered aloneness suddenly felt so lonely.

CHAPTER SEVEN

They were gone for what seemed a terribly long time.

Perhaps it wasn't so long, but to Judith, who could not find any of her many duties occupying enough to keep her from glancing through the greenhouse walls to the empty road, it was interminable. She tried everything she knew, from rearranging the seedlings to hosing down the glass walls, but she found it almost impossible to fully occupy her mind, to cleanse away all thoughts of Jason McNair. Like a bee seeking the sweet nectar of a tulip patch, he had left a subtle but potent dash of pollen in her being that refused to blow away in the springtime breeze. Or perhaps it was the nip of his stinger she was feeling as it pulsed his indelible poison into her body, making her as uncomfortable with his absence as she was with his presence.

As the sun began to lean downward toward its western cradle, into the rounded arms of the Pennsylvania foothills, Judith gazed over the delicate variegation of the meadow and thought of reasons to go to the Viguera house down the road. Let's see . . . she needed to put in an order with Peter's father for a week's groceries—Sam Viguera ran a produce warehouse. And she needed to borrow the truck so she could haul the overgrowth away from her garden area. And she needed to retrieve her book of bread recipes from Peter's mother. . . .

Excuses! All excuses to see McNair. Excuses to find out why he was in no hurry to return.

But this was ridiculous! She didn't care when he came back. Or *if* he came back, for that matter. In fact she would be delighted if he never came back at all.

And that Peter. Didn't he remember that he had a job to do? She knew he loved history and had few people who could keep up with him on it, but this was springtime and there were orders to fill. . . .

Judith sat in her rattan chair as evening crept up, gazing out the window, through delicate frothy leaves of sage and thyme that grew in far too many odd soup cans and tea tins cluttering the window and the now-golden rays of the sunset slanted against the tins in sleepy warmth. In her hands she held a mug of cappuccino that hadn't been hot for some time, forgotten by the preoccupied woman who had so meticulously created it.

Before another half hour went by, Judith found herself pacing the cabin like a caged bear, unsatisfied with anything she attempted to do to distract herself. She traded in her T-shirt for a light flannel shirt that conquered the evening's coolness, then stalked to her stereo and flipped through her record collection, finally settling on a favorite, Gordon Lightfoot, and insisted to herself that the sparkle of very proficient guitar playing and a buttery masculine voice would calm her down to her usual self.

Dinner.

Yes. She would make dinner. She was hungry anyway. And, just to be polite, just in case he walked in, she would make enough for two.

The familiar Lightfoot strains filled the air and made it as golden as the sunset on the wood of her windowsill, and Judith set her mind to the idea that Jason would roll in in plenty of time to partake of hot rice pasties.

While the rice was boiling, Judith kept wandering closer and closer to the telephone. Somehow, though, she managed to keep herself from calling the Viguera place and broadcasting to the immediate world that she was interested in Jason McNair's pointed lack of interest in her. Wasn't he supposed to be monitoring her? Changes in moods? Odd occurrences? Daily habits? Was he paying her all this money to sit by herself?

The money. Trapped. Trapped in her own house like an animal in a zoo, she was free to wander her artificial environment without the freedom to enjoy it, to flee or return at will, trapped and forced to live her life under constant observation or left in confused solitude at the whims of an unfamiliar science. Judith clenched her hands into cold white fists and was trying to bear the strain gracefully, now having also to deal with keeping the rice pasties hot and tender for much too long a time, when she heard the rented Datsun drive up the road and swing to a halt on the grass outside the cabin.

She hurried to stand up and try to look busy, which she wasn't, but not busy making him dinner, which she was.

He came in, filling the doorway imposingly, whistling a merry unknown melody as though he had nothing serious in the world to contend with. Maybe he didn't. Maybe he didn't take Judith's psychic abilities seriously at all. Maybe his interest was nothing more than a professional smokescreen, designed to make her feel as though he believed her to be genuine, while all the time he fostered doubts. He had said it himself—automatic doubts came with the specialty of psychic study.

"Good evening," he greeted with lighthearted formality.

"Hello," Judith droned, sloshing the mugful of cold cappuccino into the sink and washing it down. Desperate to appear distracted, she began poring over a hasty list of things to do tomorrow. She happened to notice that she really did have plenty to do. Why was she unable to concentrate on it?

Jason bounced a polite glance off her and made himself at home with an ease that must have been deliberate, pointedly ignoring her as she followed him with a questioning regard.

"Did you enjoy yourself?" she bridged coolly.

"Entirely. Peter is a very intelligent young man. I hardly noticed the afternoon go by. He knits an enthrallingly detailed conversation on many periods of history. I must say, I was very impressed with him. If he's not college material, I don't know who is."

"Yes, I know," Judith said frostily. "I'm arranging for a percentage of his wages to be set aside for college." *So there,* she added in the privacy of her own mind, *you don't know anything about Peter that I don't already know.*

"It won't be wasted," Jason casually observed as he settled into the easy chair and thumbed through a paperback history book Peter had lent him.

Judith blew an inaudible comment through her nostrils and turned to the kitchenette. Staunchly she served up two plates but stopped cold when, from across the room, he mentioned, "I'm glad to see you went ahead with dinner for yourself. The Viguera family fed me quite well this evening. Roast beef, au gratin potatoes, beef gravy with mushrooms . . . delicious. I feel like a stuffed goose."

Judith pressed her lips together tightly and stared down at the two full plates, her hands ice-cold with anger. Without a word she shoveled the contents of one plate into the other and sat down at the table, by herself.

Jason looked up briefly. "I see you have a big appetite tonight. I'll have to note that."

Her face reddened, she hoped not obviously, and her jaws ached as she clenched them. She remained silent, picking a fork through one rice pasty.

"Is something wrong?" he asked.

"Nothing."

"Did you have a bad day?"

"No, not really." Her words were clipped, terse. "In fact it was very nice. I enjoyed the solitude immensely."

"You don't seem too happy, Judith. Did one of those collectors call?"

"No . . ."

"Well, if they do, you can tell them they'll no longer need to harass you."

Don't remind me, Judith thought fiercely, but managed to keep silent about it.

"Anything else?" he asked.

"What?"

"Is anything else bothering you?"

His tolerance infuriated her.

"I was wondering," she began, diving headlong into the fire, "why you stayed away so long when both you and Peter have jobs to do here. I thought you were supposed to be observing me. It's a good thing I didn't have a vision or something."

"It's a vision, Judith, not a baby. You don't need help to have one."

"Your institute approached me, remember? This wasn't my idea in the first place."

He rose and moved sinuously toward her, a large animal stalking his prey.

"In deference to you, Judith, I've made a point of not intruding on your privacy at all times. For those times, I will simply request that you record on paper any visions you may have. I assumed you would think of that on your own."

She met his caustic chestnut glare. "It's not my job to record anything. When the visions end I'm glad to be rid of them. I don't need to be forcing myself to retain details for your sake, Jason."

"Then do it for your own sake. You don't like me—you've made that amply clear—and you resent my being here. Actually, for the money I'm paying you I don't much care what you like, but I do expect some cooperation from you. Now, if you don't mind, I'm going to retire

67

to the loft to record this change of moods in my 'Judith' log."

He pivoted gracefully and headed toward the loft, but turned in the entryway to the hall and crisply ordered, "By the way, don't go to bed without checking with me first. I have to begin recording a morning and night physiological calendar on you. If you do, I'll have to come in and wake you up, so be a good girl and don't force me to invade your bedchamber again."

Why did he have to remind her of that episode? Judith quivered at the recollection of his hands on her body; even Jason's imaginary hands had carried a power that transcended mere fantasy and surged into the hot folds of reality. It couldn't be real, couldn't be a sign of what was inevitably to come about—she wouldn't allow it!

But could she stop it? So far, every vision had come true.

Nervous, she finished her meal, managing only half the food on her plate and having to wrap the rest and refrigerate it for lunch tomorrow. Still, the aloneness seemed to throb at her from behind the room-filling music. She kept the stereo going continually, determined not to let Jason think she was less than fully occupied with her own interests.

For two hours there was no sign of life from the loft. When Jason finally came down, he bore an armful of what looked like—yes, it was—medical equipment. A stethoscope, a blood pressure unit, papers and record books, and a smug expression.

"Are you ready to give me some time, Judith?" he asked, and she couldn't tell if the cheerfulness was genuine or not.

Judith did not reply, but continued shaving a chunk of paraffin into thin sheets to be melted and made into the spice candles that were so popular with her clients.

Jason went on unfazed. "I'll need to have your heart rate and blood pressure every morning and night, and I'll be taking your temperature and monitoring your diet."

Snidely Judith replied, "Why, Jason, I'm sure you know a vegetarian diet is much too bland to have any real physiological effects."

Now it was Jason's turn to remain silent. He stoically flipped open a notebook and started writing, narrating as he went. "May 9, ten P.M. Subject is unaccountably irritable. Will presently attempt physiological readings, if able to approach. Applying whip-and-chair method." His brows lifted illustratively beneath the curtain of dark hair.

Judith sneered at him while he wasn't looking, but a twinge of guilt lanced her nonetheless.

"Do you know what the whip-and-chair method is, Judith?" He moved toward her, lynxlike.

"I'm not really interested."

"Well, I'm going to tell you anyway, so that you may take precautions. The whip-and-chair method is when I hold you down and tickle you under the ribs until . . . your feet fall off."

A quirkish grin tugged at Judith's lips, and, though she tried to resist it, the whole picture was so hilarious that she couldn't keep a giggle from sneaking out.

She looked up self-consciously into Jason's knowing grin. He gazed sidelong at her until she felt the redness rise in her cheeks. "There," he said. "That's the girl I remember greeting me at the door." His hand slid over hers and he drew her into the cozy side of the cabin. "Now, be a good little herbalist and let me get my readings. Sit down and relax." He wrapped the blood pressure strip around her arm and donned the stethoscope, finished that task and recorded the readings. After taking her temperature, he once again arranged the stethoscope for listening. "Please bare your chest for me."

Judith stared up at him and clutched the front of her

shirt. Suddenly she wished she had bothered to put on a bra. "I will not!" she burst.

"Oh, Judith, you're not serious. Can't we be adult about this?"

"Not that adult! I agreed to be observed, not violated."

"You agreed," he corrected, "to be investigated. I must record your physiological condition twice a day to determine if any changes coincide with psychic occurrences, and heart rate is crucial to know. Please lean back and let me do my work."

"Not a chance. Take my pulse if you want to record something." She straightened her back obstinately and offered him her wrist.

Jason cocked a trim hip. "A pulse is fine if you want to tell if someone is alive or not. It's not dependable enough for our purposes."

Her hand continued to hover before him like a cobra. "My pulse is very dependable. I've counted on it for years."

He let out an exasperated sigh and put down the stopwatch he had been using. "Okay," he breathed, "have it your own way."

She started to let her hand down, because the blood was draining out of her fingers, but gasped as Jason's hand closed harshly around her forearm and yanked her to her feet.

Yelping in shock, she was stunned to find herself flying through the air to land slung over Jason's shoulder like a sack of sea salt.

"Jason! Put me down!"

"Sorry."

"Put me down right now!"

"If you insist."

His shoulders shifted beneath her as he moved to the center of the sheepskin rug and flung her down onto it. She tried to scramble away, but his knees trapped her legs as he knelt on top of her and dug his fingertips into her rib cage.

"No!" she screamed, unable to keep the laughter down, hopelessly writhing under his grasp. "Stop it! Stop!" She heard her own laughter echo as she struggled, her eyes watering and tears tumbling down her hot cheeks.

"Do I get your heart rate?"

"No! Stop this! I mean it!"

Again his fingers plied her ribs with light but firm strokes, seeking and finding the tender ticklish spots, and she squirmed deliriously until she was breathlessly begging him to cease.

"Well?"

"Okay! Okay . . . just stop. . . ."

"Good." He arranged the stethoscope again and grasped Judith's wrists, holding both arms down on the floor over her head with one large hand.

"What are you doing?" she demanded. "Let go of my hands."

"I don't trust you."

"I don't trust you, either. Let go of my hands!"

"Stop exciting yourself or I won't get an accurate rate."

Judith bellowed, "If you were human, I'd hate you!"

"Hush, now. I don't take wood nymphs seriously."

"Don't you mock my profession!"

"Why not?" Coolly he began unbuttoning her shirt with his free hand. "You enjoy conjuring up mystical things that could be easily purchased in any neighborhood health food or craft shop. You epitomize quaintness itself."

He was infuriating her and he knew it.

"Who do you think puts the stuff in the stores so automatons like you can think they're getting back to nature?" she shrieked, arching her back in an attempt to throw him off. It was as though she was pinned under a boulder.

The middle button of her shirt slid under his fingers and

71

the front of her blouse parted to bare the creamy white valley between her breasts. Though he said nothing about it, the arousal was clear in his eyes as he realized she was wearing nothing but the shirt, and she held her breath to keep her chest from swelling like a hunting call before him.

"Really, Judith," he said, forcing himself to concentrate, "I must insist that you calm down. I have to get something concrete out of this adventure, don't I?"

Desperate to distract him from his perusal of her too-visible cleavage, she blurted, "If you're insinuating that my visions are a sham, you're vastly mistaken. I'm not some bubble-head who likes to play with witchcraft, and I'm as anxious to disbelieve the visions as you seem to be, except they're *mine* and I can't help it! Just because I deal in herbs doesn't mean I'm a nut plucked off my own vine!" She babbled angrily under his weight and grip, until she realized her writhing had tossed the edges of her shirt away to reveal the sumptuous velvety inner curves of her breasts. She froze, breathless from her own tirade, knowing that any more struggling would cast the edges of her shirt completely astray, discarding her only shield against him.

He paused for a moment and his eyes roved over the curves of her breasts. Only the tails of her shirt tucked into her jeans kept her from total humiliation. "Lovelier than I could have imagined," he murmured. Was he serious? Or was this more of his game to enrage her?

"Please don't do this," she begged quietly.

He grasped the business end of his stethoscope. "Sit still." Silently he took her heart rate, and she trembled under the cool instrument and the heat of her own emotions. "Can't you take a compliment from an appreciative gentleman?" he asked after a drawn pause.

"If I recall correctly," Judith said through gritted teeth, "no gentleman ever treated me the way you do."

"Do you expect to be treated like a debutante twirling a parasol? I'm not here to flatter your femininity."

"Thanks."

"No offense intended. Simply stating the facts."

Caustically she replied, "Nothing short of that would ever occur to you, I'm sure. And let go of my hands!"

"Done." He released her reddened wrists.

"Now get off me."

"In a moment." He carefully recorded the precious heart rate in his log.

A captive, she remained pinned beneath his considerable weight, unable to alter the situation until he finished writing, and she could tell he was stalling calculatively, enjoying every moment of his power over her.

"You think you're funny, don't you?" she asked.

"Of course." In a single graceful motion he swung to one side and freed her, remaining beside her on his knees as he coiled his stethoscope. "Funny, dashing, intelligent, and . . . have I forgotten anything?"

"Modest," she grunted. In her haste to get up she failed to notice that Jason's weight had stopped the circulation in her legs and rendered them too numb to bear her weight. Her knees buckled before her feet ever had a chance to do their job, and a tiny cry escaped her lips as she piled headlong into Jason.

His arms closed around her and together they tumbled once again to the floor, but now they were locked lengthwise against each other, eyes much too close, lips even closer.

For a moment they froze in place, Jason's arm coiled around her back, holding her to his chest in unexpected protectiveness, and he too seemed surprised to find her in his arms. Surprised, but not displeased.

When the surprise faded from his sculpted features, pleasure rose to take its place and his lips widened in a sincere smile. In a moment he was chuckling, and Judith felt the low vibrations up and down the length of his body against hers. Then, hardly realizing it, she was laughing too.

It seemed folly to struggle, and they laughed as the ice shattered and floated away between them.

After a few moments, though, the laughter began to fade.

Suddenly he was closer, his lips parted slightly, their eyes melting together in an unexpected blaze of desire. Was it happening? Was it another "dream"? Could it be true that Judith's own lips were parting, throbbing to feel the heat of his?

Her hand crept up his chest and finally slid around his neck as he drew her nearer with the pressure of his arm around her shoulders. His lips closed on hers, moist and hot, growing hotter still. Greedily his mouth spread over hers, forcing a muffled groan of pleasure to rise in her throat. She braced her heels against the floor and arched herself into the hard curve of his prone body. Her mind seemed impervious to sensible thoughts, instead filling with flashes of electricity that ran up her legs and down her spine. A tiny echo inside her head called to her to refuse his touch, but his seeking lips and crushing embrace made demands upon her that swept all defenses aside.

Jason's long dark eyelashes brushed against Judith's cheek as he worked his mouth against her, his tongue exploring the sensuous feminine drive of hers. Yes—she was as much a woman as he had guessed upon his first sight of her. She moved against him with eagerness he could only have wished for, their breath coming in short gasps and long rushes, heavier and deeper with every moment, with every wave of passion that surged through them.

For Judith, all she had known about men, about feelings of desire and need and caring, was redefining itself. What once had been rejection became fiery acceptance. Suspicion and doubt metamorphosed into wild passion, as hot, moist kisses ran the length of her throat to the pulsing skin of her breasts. Soon Jason's feverish face was buried in taut cleavage. Her breasts quivered beneath his fingertips as he freed them from the rims of the open shirt, his stiff tongue circling a nipple and then tracing the fleshy wholeness that made Judith the goddess of nature he thought her. Her hands twined into the confines of his belt line, drawing up the tail of his shirt to explore finally his heaving side and the hard tension of his back. Control was a word without meaning, and though a ghost called to her to push him back, to remember what a man really was beneath professions of love, Judith had ears only for the anxious breaths that signaled Jason's uncontrollable arousal.

They entered the void and crossed the boundary to no-return, committed to a promise neither had planned for. Thrusting aside all emotional defenses, they plunged headlong into forbidden, age-old games of conquest, unable and unwilling to turn back.

Outside, far away and forgotten, the sun slid behind foggy mountains and settled into a purple haze, as though it understood a time for darkness.

CHAPTER EIGHT

She awoke in her own bed. For a time she was certain it had been a dream. Only a dream. A dream with all the tangible realities of a psychic vision.

Oh, such a dream . . . was this the kind of wonderful womanliness the girls in college has gossiped about? Could it be that this was the feeling that had fired their youth with such anxious vitality? If it had been a dream, Judith wished to sleep again, to scale those silky heights, the touch, the scent of a man in the throes of love. Love for *her.*

She stretched languidly, her arms curling around her head, tangling in her hair—but that wasn't *her* arm—

She moaned softly and opened her eyes.

In the dim lemony haze of early morning, her sleep-heavy eyes traced the large form of a muscular shoulder. A thick arm arched over her breasts to tuck under the back of her neck. Jason's face was turned away on the pillow; he was lying face down, his rich brown hair tousled. He was lying almost on top of her, coiled protectively over her long body, his breathing the steady drawn rhythm of deep sleep, of a man quite satisfied.

Most of his body was uncovered, though Judith was tangled in the cottony folds of her favorite quilt. His legs were sprawled over hers with a childlike abandon, his toes hanging over the end of the mattress.

"Oh, God," Judith murmured. "Oh, no." Like a lamb

facing slaughter, she slowly came to consciousness, slowly accepting the facts that surrounded her. But there was little sincerity in her voice as she mumbled a self-curse. Nothing could dull the biggest fact of all. She had wanted him last night. Wanted him beyond the limits of anything she had ever desired. And, like a foolish child, she had succumbed to his game—in fact, helped him win.

Her body grew cold as self-awareness returned, and a stiffness came over her limbs.

Even in his slumber Jason sensed it.

With a groan of contentment he rolled over and slid his arms around her waist, pulling her against his bare body as his long legs dug through the covers to coil around hers. With a deep sigh, he once again drifted into total sleep.

Pinned there with only her increasingly stormy thoughts, Judith fought to regain her suspicion of men, her old knowledge of their capricious nature. She tried with all her might to be angry, to be hateful. To despise Jason McNair.

She failed miserably. No man could have feigned the tender intimacy that had driven Jason last night. No man was actor enough to portray that kind of eager need and sensitivity of spirit.

Rough gentility . . . was there such a thing?

Yes . . . and Judith had found it. Satisfaction kept her heart beating a slow, drowsy drum, and yet her mind continued to tumble. A small pit of hardness grew in her stomach.

Fear entered the picture.

The sun was warm on the cabin, but it couldn't draw the pit of chill from Judith's soul. In spite of it, she felt a surge of self-confidence, of independence. Last night hadn't been just for Jason. It had been a gift from Judith to herself, to quench a need to give and receive love. She tried to promise herself that it wouldn't happen again.

77

Somehow, fate had its way and she had made love to the mysterious man whom her mind had pictured so intimately. Now it was all over, and she could recapture control over her life.

At least, that was how she planned it as she worked feverishly in the cabin cellar, crushing and packaging dried parts of various culinary herbs for shipment at the end of the week, only two days away. Since Jason arrived, she had been so distracted she had hardly accomplished anything. There were potpourris to make, herb vinegars to bottle, soap to mold and wrap, tea bags to fill—would she ever finish in time? She had lots of orders; if only her business was big enough to absorb the money she was getting from Jason's institute. If only she could tell him to go away, now, before they dug themselves deeper into the hole that had tripped her like a cantering filly last night. All she needed was to be buried under emotional commitment to a man!

She had risen quietly, stealthily this morning, not wanting Jason to wake. She would stall colliding with him as long as possible today. She had gone immediately to work, determined not to make breakfast for him; she didn't want to appear as a pseudohousewife, available for his comfort and satisfaction. If he wanted breakfast, he could just as well get his own. He hadn't had any trouble taking the initiative last night!

If only his touch hadn't been so tender, his whispered words so sweet. If only he hadn't been so kind, so strong, so gentle with her. If only she hated talking to him and listening to his replies.

But she didn't. The sound of his voice was a mellow power that attracted her like a magnet. It had shocked her how much she had missed him when he spent all day with Peter, and how she had wished he would return. Had he really colored her life so much? Could it be that the world actually contained a man whom she could love *and* trust?

Could she learn to have faith in a man after all the agony and superficiality men had brought into her life and her poor mother's? Judith thought of her mother now, in whom her wretched father had had such a blindly devoted wife, a wife he had sorely abused in the witness of his little daughter, a child who would bear permanent emotional scars because of a man's idea of "love." But desire and love were two different things; if Judith's father had left her nothing, he had left her that knowledge. Then her erstwhile fiancé had drilled the truth of it home, and caused her to shrug off the hopes of finding a man to believe in, caused her to swear off all pursuit of such a creature altogether.

She was wrestling with her feelings, and losing, when strong arms caught her around the waist and she was jerked back against a firm body. She gasped and shuddered as lips ran from her ear to her shoulder.

"You startled me . . ." she said noncommittally.

"Why?" he murmured in that low, silky tone. "Were you expecting someone else?"

She tried to continue stuffing the preprinted Calico Patch bags with herbs, but his arms tightened beneath her breasts and were indeed distracting. He nosed her hair aside and playfully licked her ear.

"What if I was?" she toyed idiotically, then wished she could catch back the words. Quickly she added, "You certainly can't be possessive already."

"Why not? I can't help fostering an emotional attachment to a woman who makes me act like . . . I'm under a spell. You do that to me, you know, Judith. You're a witch after all." He released her waist, leaving the skin warm and moist beneath the blue halter top and flannel over-blouse, grasped her shoulders, and spun her into his arms again, kneading her against his body as far down his long frame as he could reach. "Let me take you away from

79

all this, my beauty," he rumbled in a playful tone. "To breakfast, at least."

"But I have—"

"Nothing that can't wait, I'm sure. Later we'll find Peter and we'll finish your day's work together. But for now, I want you all to myself."

It was difficult to resist him. He was quite attractive in gray slacks and a black knit shirt that creased tightly around his torso, but she gave it a game try.

"Jason—"

"No excuses." He caught her mouth in his, dazing her into submission again, though she raised her hands in useless protest and in a moment he had her bodily off the floor and was carrying her upstairs.

"I don't want to go to breakfast," she protested half-heartedly. "I usually fast one day a week—"

"This isn't the day." He lowered her legs until her feet touched the floor. "Put on something nice and meet me at the car in five minutes."

Despite herself, Judith hesitated only a moment before hustling to obey him. In fact, she found herself humming as she vigorously brushed her hair and pushed it back with two tortoiseshell combs. The effect was a volume of downy tresses cascading down her back, leaving her large eyes and cheekbones to take the stage. She selected a flouncy lavender peasant shirt and belted it with a plain rope from which various sea shells dangled. She felt light on her feet, yet in spite of it all she still couldn't beat down the nagging doubt that kept her stomach knotted. Was it her imagination, or was he always in control? Even this light-headedness she was feeling, even his good mood, due to delight with his conquest of her, seemed to be utterly under Jason's power.

Well . . . maybe it was just hollow suspicion on her part. Maybe it really was time to give manhood a second chance.

She dabbed on lip gloss of a peachy shade and stepped back to take in the whole image of her reflection in her dresser mirror.

Pleased, she said, "Hm. Maybe he's better for me than I thought." She tossed her hair to fluff it up after the brushing, and tried to smile, to see if her lip gloss was even.

The smile didn't last long. It was artificial. No matter how happy she wanted to feel, she couldn't completely kill the knot of doubt, or keep it from showing up on her face. No matter how hard she tried or how flattered she was by Jason's attention, she couldn't fight the tremor in her smile or the tension in her eyes. She could only hope it wouldn't show too much, or that a facade of security could overshadow it.

With those thoughts nipping at her heels, she hurried to join Jason at the car.

The drive through the Pennsylvania countryside, now speckled with verdant nubs on every tree and bush, made Judith forget her doubts and become enraptured with the view.

Jason was like a strutting peacock as he drove and chatted with her, and though it was imposing, it made her more aware that his puffed-up vanity had come at her expense.

The silver Datsun broke out of the tightly woven hillside road and drove out into a wider expanse of rolling countryside. The panorama was of velvety patches of verdure, emerald here, jade there, overlapped with swatches of shamrock and apple greens. The bright sun made each shade double on itself and become even more deep and resonant. Birds swooped across an indelibly blue sky, on their way north, winging with anticipation that called at them. Judith was unable to resist their appeal.

She thought of Peter; he was as wild as springtime and just as dependable. He had come bounding across the meadow, the shortcut from his house, his eyes widening as he saw Judith "all dressed up" and preparing to get into the car with Jason.

"What's going on?" he had asked.

"We're going on a date," Jason replied steadily.

"We're going to breakfast," Judith promptly corrected. "What about work?"

Guilt nibbled at Judith's good mood. "Well . . . do me a favor and flip through this week's orders. Do what you can, and we'll be back in time for me to put in a long day. Then you can have tomorrow off."

Peter shrugged, puzzled. "Okay," he said. "Hey, Jace, here's one. Who defeated Bonnie Prince Charlie of Scotland and where? And when?"

"Oh, come on, Peter. You can provide a better challenge than that," Jason admonished. "Charles Edward Stuart of Scotland was defeated at Culloden by the Duke of Cumberland. The date was sometime in April of 1746. I've even been there myself. Now, you tell me the name of Alexander the Great's horse."

"Easy. Bucephalas. Who was—"

"Excuse me," Judith interrupted. "I have work to do, so hurry the history lesson up a bit, would you?"

"The lady has spoken, Peter."

"Yeah. I'll be thinking of something to stump you with, Jace. I'm gonna get you, sooner or later."

At this, Jason had flicked his cocoa gaze to Judith, added a sly twisting grin, and said heavily, "Nonsense. No one ever gets me."

Judith had been chilled by his sauciness, distressed by the insinuation that he could have anything, anyone he wanted, but always on his own terms. One-way arrangements—Jason's way.

Restlessness manifested itself now in tiny beads of perspiration trickling down Judith's throat. She nearly jumped out the window when Jason reached across the console and squeezed her thigh with possessive intimacy. "Something the matter?"

"Just a little warm," she said, rolling her window down and hanging her elbow out to catch the breeze.

"Warm and nothing else?"

"What else?" She tried to shrug.

"You seem preoccupied. Are you having second thoughts?"

"About what?"

"Judith," he said with a little huff of exasperation, "about last night. About me. You can't possibly regret it." He turned slightly sideways in the seat, resting his wrist on top of the steering wheel and hanging the other arm across her shoulders. Why did this car have to be so small, she despaired.

His loaded gaze was intoxicating, and Judith's body surged with remembrance. "At least," he went on, "you didn't seem regretful when I took you in my arms and I . . ."

"Please—" she intoned. "Jason . . . I'm not sure yet how I feel about it. I haven't had a man around or a . . . relationship . . . for so long, I don't know what I'm feeling."

His straight lips twisted again, this time into a sardonic glower. "I see," he said curtly. "And I was so sure you had felt the same as I did about last night."

"Yes, I noticed you were sure," she snapped back at him. Instantly she wished the words had gone out the window, unheard.

His voice cooled her off plenty. "I see I was laboring under an assumption. I'm very sorry if my attentions caused you any confusion, but all I had to go on was your willingness last night."

"Stop talking about me like that! I'm not a puppet!"

"I never said—"

"Please take me home."

"We're going to breakfast."

"I'd rather not."

"Regardless, we're going."

"You don't own me, Jason. I may be psychic, but I'm not stupid."

"You're not an unfeeling ice cube, either. There must be some way to get through to your heart, and I'm going to find it."

Seething, Judith knew that half of her anger and the exasperation she was feeling stemmed from the fact that Jason McNair had already touched her heart, deeper than she was willing to admit even to herself. She still felt the strings of last night reverberating deep within her. "My heart is my own," she lied artfully, "for me to give or keep as I so elect. And I do not elect."

He had already conquered her body, and plainly meant to go on conquering her, heart and soul, until every defense was melted. And would he give her the same devotion he professed to have given his young wife before she died? No, Judith couldn't imagine it. She was far from a child of eighteen who would have felt honored by the attentions of a man like Jason McNair. She was her own person, and she would control her own life, her own love. If only Jason could respect that, perhaps she could overcome her skepticism about men and allow the wonderful sensations he caused in her to be freely expressed.

But as long as his attitude was like this, there was little chance that she could find the peace in love that she had found in solitude.

Her thoughts were broken as the car pulled onto the gravel shoulder of the road and shuddered to a halt. Judith hardly breathed as Jason left the car and stalked around to her side, where he yanked the door open and reached for her.

She recoiled slightly, but not enough, and in an instant she was out of the car, clamped tightly between his viselike hands, staring into the dangerous hardness of his eyes as they darkened.

"I have something to apprise you of, my dear," he said, his voice stung with omen. "I don't give my attentions easily, and when I do I expect them to be taken graciously."

"You mean 'gratefully,' don't you?" she dared to remark. She wasn't worried about his mounting anger; even in the short time they had known each other, she was sure he was not a man who expected a woman to suffer his anger in silence. Yet there was an animal lurking behind those stormy eyes, an animal to whom Judith was prey. As threatening as he was, standing there crushing her arms in his grip and blazing that chestnut warning down at her, Judith couldn't resist the hateful truth: he was more alluring, more captivating, more magnetic than ever before.

And he was bewitched with her, she could tell, beckoned by the sheer adventure of her daring to defy him. His eyes narrowed ominously and his tongue ran across his slightly parted lips as a hint of deviltry tugged his expressive mouth. A satanic shadow washed over his features.

The greenery around them blurred as he crushed her against him and his mouth took cruel possession of her, his tongue diving into the warm moistness within. A protest rose in her throat, but became a groan of pleasure before it ever surfaced.

It wasn't a kiss of love, it was a brand of possession. But despite the resentment that rose in some rational part of her mind, his rough embrace had the same effect on her as his most tender caress of the previous night—stirring up a muddle of passion, excitement, and an unquestioning acceptance of her destiny in this man's arms.

Light flashed behind her eyes as all common sense succumbed to the power of Jason's warmth and strength, engulfing her totally. And for a moment, she thought that was all it was.

Then she pulled away and put one hand over her eyes, the other pressing against his chest.

Lights—red ones—continued flashing.

Jason slackened his grip on her arms, but sensed her unsteadiness and didn't let go.

"What is it?" he asked, suddenly the cool professional. "What do you see?"

"I-I think it's a fire . . . no . . . an ambulance . . ."

"Relax and let it happen. Try to encourage the vision instead of fighting it."

She broke away from him and shook away the image. "I can't . . . why would I be seeing an ambulance? It can't mean anything good. . . ."

"Are you sure that's what it was? Could it have been anything else?" He was holding onto her wrist now, but not out of concern. He was, she realized, taking her pulse pragmatically, observing the seconds tick off on his digital watch.

"I don't think so . . . oh, I don't know!" Judith said, distressed. "Sometimes I can't tell what they are until after it happens." As it was, this time the image was much less distinct than any she had experienced before.

"So you expect this to 'come true'?"

"Why not?" she sighed, stomping onto the grass. "All the others did! Oh, what is it this time?" She fought back a swell of tears successfully, but couldn't cool the redness in her cheeks or the fear in her eyes. She *was* becoming some kind of ghoul!

"Don't overreact, Judith. There's no point in becoming hysterical."

"I'm not hysterical."

"Get back in the car and we'll get going." He was calmly recording the whole incident in a notepad that had been tucked in his back pocket.

86

Judith closed her eyes briefly, then opened them again, quickly, because the darkness in there suddenly bothered her. She didn't want to get back in the car at all. Who knew where she would end up? Who could tell what terrible happening her mind had just hinted at? Was the warning for herself? Would she end up in a hospital again? Or was it for someone else? Whose life had just flashed before her? That was the worst part of her "ability"; she seldom had enough to go on to actually change a potential tragedy. It was rare for her to recognize much of anything in her own visions.

She took a deep breath. They couldn't exactly stay out here all day, could they? With a sigh, she turned and went toward the car.

Then it hit her.

Could it be that the warning was about Jason? She found herself staring at him as he wrote in his little book, standing there beside the car with the sun shimmering on his dark hair, creating highlights on his muscular arms and shoulders beneath the snug black shirt. His magnetism struck her again, along with the impact of what it would mean to her if he was injured. It was startling how much she was affected by that idea. . . .

With so little to go on, she didn't voice her fear as she obediently got back in the car, and moments later they were wheeling down the road again, each preoccupied with silent thought.

It was breathtaking how fast—how soon—it happened.

Not ten minutes later, they were winding down a narrow foothill road, swinging around a typical curve with mountain on one side and a drop-off on the other, when Judith inhaled sharply and uttered a cry of warning.

Before them, a Croft Emergency ambulance wheeled crazily around the bend in *their* lane!

The ambulance lights flashed wildly as Jason swerved the car and the ambulance driver did the same. They shot

87

by each other, but it was too late for Jason to recover. The car lanced through foliage and scraped into a pod of young trees, coming to a halt only inches from the edge of the ravine.

The only sounds were the snaps of a few twigs as supple branches settled back into place.

CHAPTER NINE

There was a slight ringing in Judith's ears, but she managed to find the courage to open her eyes, which had clamped shut in the face of certain doom, to see that the car had settled securely enough away from the edge of the ravine. It wasn't much of a ravine anyway, but who wanted to explore it in a tumbling car?

Afraid to look, Judith turned to see Jason shaking his head and rubbing his left temple.

"You all right?" he asked her, a stray hand reaching her way.

"Yes . . . your head . . ."

"It's no big deal. I collided with the window. Judith, you really *did* see an ambulance."

"I told you I did," she began, then hesitated. Of course, he hadn't believed her.

"Let's get out of here." Jason nudged his door open gingerly, testing to see if the car would jar loose and slide down the incline. It didn't even budge, so he got out and helped Judith climb out the driver's side just as the ambulance swung back around the bend. Two attendants jumped out and ran at them full tilt.

"Are you folks okay?" the driver asked frantically. "I misjudged the turn—couldn't stay in my own lane."

"You sure did misjudge," Jason said dryly. "But we're fine."

"Listen, I've got an emergency at Cliff Ridge. I can dispatch another ambulance—"

"No, not necessary. You go on your way."

"You're sure?"

"Yes."

"Okay, if you say so, but I'll be back this way, and if you can't get your car out by then, I'll dispatch a tow truck and we'll pick up the fee. I'm awful sorry—" He continued apologizing until he and his partner were back in the ambulance and once again rushing out of sight.

"Well," Jason huffed, looking at her with a strangely potent regard, "there's your ambulance. And may I say I am amazed. I owe you an apology for doubting you."

Yes, you do, she thought, but managed to take his apology gracefully. "What about your head? And the car?"

"Never mind my head," he said, taking her by the shoulders again, more gently this time. "I'm more interested in your head. You may have saved our lives and those of the ambulance attendants, not to mention the person they're on their way to help."

"I don't understand," Judith said slowly. "What do you mean? You were driving."

"Yes, but my mind was on ambulances. I wasn't half as startled to see that ambulance coming at us as I would ordinarily have been. I was also keyed into the idea that *something* was going to happen. I've seen a few convincing psychics, but it's been a long time since I've encountered anything as tightly woven as what just happened to us." He strode pensively to the roadside and thought aloud, "I'm going to get my assistant down here to help me run some tests on you and analyze the data. I think you're actually going to earn your stipend, Judith."

Judith slumped against the car. "Thanks," she muttered, disgruntled. *How perfectly charming. How divine. Thanks a lot. Maybe I can cast a spell on the car and it'll float up onto the pavement.* It gave her no pleasure to be reminded of the great need she had for the money he represented. At least his amorous attentions had distracted her from that sad reality. But he had not forgotten why he was here, or that she had no choice but to allow him to stay.

The car had posed some problem, but a little judicious wheel spinning and good use of Jason's burly muscle power against the front bumper eventually urged the vehicle free of the grass and back onto the shoulder, where it bit into the gravel and drew itself out to the road. That made Judith feel somewhat better; at least she didn't have to see the ambulance again, and she and Jason didn't have to wait for help.

He still insisted on taking her to breakfast, though he did most of the talking, involved now with getting his assistant into the picture and diving into some hard-core psychic research. To Judith it seemed tiresome, exhausting in the anticipation of having her mind picked apart, as well as clouding up her daily business schedule with another demanding commitment. The whole morning, in fact, had served only to muddle her emotional state even more. How could her life have complicated itself so quickly?

Once home again, she plunged headlong into her work, and worked long into the night, outrunning both Peter and Jason, who eventually gave up on her and went to bed. Peter fell asleep in the hammock, a common occurrence that his parents were used to, and Judith assumed Jason had gone back to the loft.

Only when she too finally ran out of energy did she also discover the extent of Jason's possession of her.

After showering, she dragged herself into her bedroom on legs that ached with exhaustion and was dully surprised to find her bed unmade. Usually she at least yanked the covers up so that they wouldn't create a lumpy mess.

91

She shrugged at herself, too tired to care, and let her robe slip unnoticed to the carpet.

Her bed was cool and inviting as she slid neatly under the fluffy quilt. The quilt was about a million years old, with rips and stray threads everywhere, but it always provided just enough warmth for any season of the year. She snuggled down into the familiar cradle of her bed and squirmed toward the center of the mattress.

There, she encountered solid matter.

A quick breath shot into her lungs and she froze.

The solidity beside her was warm and intriguing, a mound of slow-breathing magnetism.

"Jason . . ." she blurted without thinking.

He groaned peacefully and made a single luxurious move that drew her into his grasp and coiled a bear hug around her.

A violent surge freed her. "What are you doing in my bed?"

Shaken rudely to consciousness, Jason raised his head. "Huh?"

"How dare you presume you're welcome in my bed!"

Still drowsy, he answered, "I just assumed—"

"Yes, you did *assume*. Please also assume that I will invite you here when and *if* I decide to."

"So we're back to that, are we?" he grumbled brusquely. Drearily he sat up and pushed the covers from his naked body. "Have it your way. I'm not going to humble myself to you, Judith." Moonlight came in the window and washed a chalky maze of shadows and highlights on his fine torso. Judith tried to keep her eyes from roving along the edges of those shadows, but masculinity was showing itself to her in many more facets than she had ever seen it before.

Jason took a few deep breaths and ran his fingers through his hair in a distracted motion. With a muffled sigh, he sat on the edge of the bed with his back to her.

"You know how I feel about you, and in spite of what you say, Judith, I think you must feel . . . something for me. I can't force you to trust me or to believe, as I do, that there's something real and rare and very beautiful between us. . . ." The low tone of his voice trailed off in an undisguised note of desperation and longing. Judith felt the sadness of his soul piercing her own, warming a place within her that had been cold and jealously guarded for far too long. Still, she did not allow herself to speak.

He stood up and flexed his shoulders, sending a strange, tremulous desire through her as the moonlight shimmered along the lines of his muscular form. "I don't give many second chances, my love," he warned softly. And it was the softness of his words that affected her.

Without totally throwing off his sleepiness, he made his way to the end of the bed, heading for the hallway, not hurrying.

Regret plunged through Judith. How could she turn him away? What harm had he done to her? What ill besides bringing a distant dream of love into her life? *Hadn't she wanted him, too?*

"Wait—" she gasped. "I . . ."

He paused at the door, half facing her, twisted just enough at the waist to tilt his shoulders slightly and allow him to question her with a pensive, expectant look. The moonlight was faint across the room, delineating a silvery line from his shoulders down the sinewy back, over well-knit buttocks and thighs to steely calves where the windowsill cast a line of darkness.

His gaze rested on the soft gray shadows of her breasts and the milky curves of the body he had caressed, on her endless hair as it rested against white shoulders, on the side of her face that was silvery in the moonlight as she hovered in quandary.

A tangible silence stretched between them.

"Please," she whispered finally, "come back . . ."

There was no distance to cover. Their arms locked around each other, drinking in the sensations with eager thirst.

"Oh, Judith," he grunted roughly, "I need you close to me so very much." Breathless gasps sputtered from his lips as they nibbled a wet trail under her ear. She yielded to his impatient hands as they traced hot trails on her back, her graceful milky body becoming velvety in the intimate ripeness of his desire.

"Make love to me," she whispered with a deliciously urgent quiver. She arched her back and let her head drift backward, inviting his tongue to probe her throat, freeing her breasts to rise between their bodies fetchingly.

He pressed her down onto the bed, his knee gently separating her creamy thighs, and he responded uncontrollably as she placed her hands on his and encouraged the wild probing of his fingers. Her body engorged itself with the sweet fire of his touch, his hands tracing intimate pictures from her breasts to her taut abdomen and below, molding her flesh with expert fingers. Their hearts pounded a cadence of passion and there was no clothing to disguise the extent of his excitement or the ripeness of her arousal. Their limbs became a tangled web, straining against its own fibers, aching for that one tantamount victory that slipped into their reach.

So . . . she loved him. She knew now. And she had learned to speak the words that triggered the sorcery of Jason McNair—the key to her own bewitching power.

The next few days were like a romp through a childhood wish.

Judith was giddy with joy at Jason's presence, and he too seemed enraptured with their togetherness, their mutual contentment. Judith and Peter worked hard during the days to fill her orders, and Jason plunged with interest into helping them. There was much laughter and

94

much loving, and Judith experienced a sensation of wholeness within herself that, she realized, had been sadly lacking. She submitted to Jason's psychical testing with hopefulness now, hoping to rid herself of the abnormality so that she could get on with her life and attend to her love of him without distraction.

Jason seemed happy to tag along with her as she went about her business, and she understood what he had meant about this being a vacation for him as well as a professional stint. He went along with her the morning she trekked down to the river to collect stalks of wild flowers that grew there, relishing the sunny, moist, mossy riverbanks where they grew in abundance.

"You're a slave driver, Longfellow," he complained as he adjusted two large wicker baskets in his arms, each cluttered with choice harvests of chamomile, calendula, dandelions, tansy, lavender, and wild thyme. Some of the plants grew naturally, but many of them were descendants of perennials Judith had planted, hoping they would catch, settle, and reproduce each season. "Don't you ever get tired of plodding through this stuff?"

"I can't afford to get tired of it," she said over her shoulder. "It's my livelihood. After a while, the novelty wears off, and awhile after that the tedium goes away and it all settles down to a comfortable routine."

He plunked the baskets down among a bed of dandelions and reached for her arm. "Let's take a break." He pulled her toward him and dropped full length onto the mossy bank. "Please, you beautiful slave driver."

"Jason, I realize these outings may look like a frolic, but it's time for work."

He grasped both her wrists. "Mutiny in the ranks." His leg coiled behind her knees and she yelped as she plunged forward and down to land sprawled atop his rough form. "Better, much better," he murmured, caressing her back with long strokes.

"Do men always get their way like you do?" Judith questioned, trying to regain some semblance of balance, but not trying too hard.

"Always," he responded huskily, "especially if there's motivation like you around."

She planted a kiss on his chin. "Flattery will get you everywhere."

"Just where I wanted to go." His fingers explored the base of her neck, twining through the soft waves of her hair as it cascaded like sea waves over his arms. The sun glittered in the strands, then raced to shine against her reflection in his eyes as he snuggled a space for her close against him in the flowers.

"I'd forgotten," he sighed as he guided her head into the crook of his neck.

"What did you say?"

A ghost of memory crossed his strong features. He twirled a strand of her hair between his fingers and seemed not to hear her. "Hm? Oh . . . I was just thinking."

"Of what?"

"Myself." He sighed again, deeply this time. "After Lesley died, I never thought another woman could break through the pain of losing her." He turned his face until he could seek out her face and hold it in his solemn gaze. "It never occurred to me that I would want someone like I want you. I thought love was over for me . . . until you."

In passionate empathy Judith caressed his throat and ran her fingers down the firmness of his chest. She felt privileged to lie here in this man's arms, couldn't help but feel lucky herself, lucky to have discovered a trustworthy, loving man before it was too late for her ever to love again, before she built up a fortress around herself and her emotions.

Jason's free hand sought and found the tender skin beneath her arm that rounded into her breast, and he cupped the fullness and caused a thrill to rush into her even through the fabric of her camisole. His great strength was reined by tenderness as he strained to reach her lips with his, and their excitement surged as his tongue invaded her parting lips and his hands caressed her, speaking to her of emotions for which there are no words.

"Oh, Jason, I've never felt like this," she sighed as he broke off the kiss and observed her as though he wanted to memorize every inch of her creamy skin. He drank in the sight of her, framed there in wild flowers.

"It's been a lifetime for me," he said quietly, tightening his embrace on her. "I never imagined this would happen when I decided to take over your investigation. Life is full of surprises." He settled back into the flowers, his legs spreading out over the mossy riverbank as he snuggled her long form very close against his body.

Love quickened within Judith like a surely kindling fire. How could she ever have been so cynical about men? Was she so shallow that a couple of bad experiences had damaged her attitude toward all men? Well, Jason had proven her wrong. She was certain of this as she pressed her face into the crook of his neck and nuzzled his ear, registering tiny tremors of desire rippling across his skin.

A huge willow waved its budding skirt along the riverbank, offering some shade from the brightness of the sun as it glinted through new leaves.

"What makes me different?" Judith asked impulsively, surprised that she felt secure enough of herself to ask that question. "You must have met women more beautiful than I am in all these years."

"Maybe," he said evasively. "I confess, a beautiful woman is difficult to resist. . . . Don't you think of yourself as beautiful?"

She shrugged. "I don't think much about it, living out here where it doesn't matter much. I suppose I'm lucky enough not to be actively ugly—"

Jason rolled his head and laughed, a hearty laugh that

echoed in her ear against his chest. "Lucky, yes, that's it. You barely sneak in under the wire of physical acceptability." He lifted his head on his hand. "Judith, you little sorceress, have you no appreciation for your own loveliness?"

She grinned. "You're making me blush."

"And rightfully so." He leaned over, his body tightening on hers, his hand pressing the firm abdomen and moving up the planes of her ribcage, under the camisole, to nestle beneath the fold of her breast. His voice became a seductive rumble deep in his throat. "You damned well better blush for what you do to me!"

Blood rushed to Judith's head as he pinned her to the submissive wild flowers with a furious kiss that was as playful as it was passionate. His clinging cotton shirt stretched over straining muscles. She felt her nipples harden and press against the camisole's fabric, aching to feel the soft brushes of his tongue and the heaviness of his hands in eager exploration.

"We're not getting much work done," she murmured breathily.

"May the world wither around us before we choose work over this. Besides," he said between sweeps of his moist lips against her skin, "I have the boss's permission."

In a rush of gaiety, Judith squirmed beneath him and wriggled out of his grasp. "The boss is no easy catch, mister," she laughed.

"Hey!" Jason's protest followed her as she grabbed a basket and dashed down the riverbank. In a trice he was after her, dodging the big willow's apron of greenery and chasing a woodland creature whose curtain of waist-length hair flew behind her in a blaze of sunlight. "You she-devil!"

They followed the river in a delightful marathon that Judith won only because she knew every inch of the ragged shoreline and knew where all the hidden paths were that made it easy to hurry over tangled roots and thorny patches. Each time she glanced back at Jason, she caught the shine of reckless desire in his eyes and the provocative grin in response to her tease.

When she came to the "bridge," a half-rotted log of oak long ago fallen across the river, she paused in the middle to check the distance between them.

There was nothing but the rustle of spring branches in the river breeze.

"Jason?" She shaded her eyes and scanned the river-bank. "Where are you?"

There was no answer.

"Jason?" She called again, louder. What could have happened to him? A dozen possibilities sprang into her mind. Had he slipped on the mossy rocks and hurt himself? Perhaps he was tangled in the thorny overgrowth, or—

She made her way slowly back over the oak log, her mind tumbling with misfortunes that could have befallen him. This countryside had snakes to offer, and loose footing, and badger holes—

At once a force caught her knees and a scream burst from her throat. She twisted furiously and coiled her arms around a welcome neck, lost her balance totally, and plunged into the cool rushing water of the river, dragging Jason with her.

They splashed and sputtered and managed to get to their feet on the muddy river floor. Jason was drenched to the waist, and Judith was completely soaked from head to toe.

"R-r-r-r!" Jason bellowed as the coldness of the water penetrated his jeans. "That wasn't in my game plan."

"How *could* you sneak up on me! Oh, it's cold!" Judith shivered and pressed the water from her camisole as she stood knee-deep in the shallow water. "You stinker . . . I was worried about you and this is what I get for it."

"I wish I had a camera," Jason murmured, leaning against the old tree bridge and running his gaze along the view provided by the wet camisole.

"Don't try to flatter me, you male chauvinist piglet, you. Look at my flowers!" She rescued the basket from becoming the next *Titanic,* but the carefully chosen flower harvest was making a little logjam against a stray branch several yards downriver.

"I think I hate you again," she said flatly.

"Then I'll have to win you again, won't I?" He started toward her, but she stumbled back.

"Don't push your luck, clown."

"Actually, Judith, I was only going to help you to shore."

Her hair drooled chilly water down her back, but she couldn't help letting the smile break through her facade. "I definitely hate you again."

"I was right about you, my love," he said as he grasped her hand and waded toward the bank. "You're a witch. You used to be a cat, but you changed yourself into a seductress. Like a cat, though, you still hate to get wet."

"It's not the wet," she said through chattering teeth, "it's the fact that the river is still back in December even though the rest of us have moved into springtime. Oh, how I just hate you."

"Allow me." He climbed onto dry land and reached for her. When they were both standing on terra firma, Jason coiled an arm around her. "Let me warm you up. Between me and the sun, we'll have you warm in no time."

"If I remember correctly," she shivered, "it was something along those lines that got me like this in the first place. I'm going b-back to the cabin to ch-change clothes." Miserably she put the saturated basket over a bush to dry.

Jason stepped back and ran a long look over her body— a look that could have dried her clothes if he'd been two inches closer. "My, my," he breathed approvingly, "you are spectacular when you're cold and wet."

Exasperated, Judith was uncomfortable enough to beat down the twinge of excitement and found little amusement in his observation as a breeze ran down the meadow and chilled her to the bone. She clamped her arms around herself, careful to cover the obvious evidence of her discomfort.

He laughed and shook his head. "Come on, mermaid. I'll swim you back to the cave."

In half an hour she was huddled in a blanket, watching Jason warm some milk for hot cocoa. "Still cold?" he asked, his tone of voice somewhat lacking in sympathy. He had changed his wet jeans for a pair of slim brown slacks exactly the color of his hair, and Judith found herself watching the minute movements of his body distractedly.

"Quit laughing at me behind your eyes, Jason McNair. Don't think I can't see that wicked little grin you've been hiding from me."

"Who? Me?"

"Yes, you."

"Madame, you cut me to the quick. Would I take advantage of your admittedly hilarious situation?"

She bulleted him a glare. "I should have let you drown."

"In four feet of water? I doubt I was in much danger." He handed her a steaming cup of hot chocolate, then sat with her at the table. "You look oddly appealing sitting there like a blanket Indian with your hair drying into weird curlicues."

Judith kicked his shin under the table.

"Ow," he said, grinning painlessly.

She raked a hand through her hair. "Yuck. It's actually sticky, isn't it?"

"Yes. In fact, I see strands of green slime here, and here—"

101

She batted his hand away. "Stop reminding me! That's it. I'm taking a shower."

Before she could get up, his hand pressed her shoulder and kept her seated with controlled strength. "Get warm inside first. Finish your hot chocolate."

"Now who's the slave driver?" She shot him a disgusted grin and was rewarded with a firm kiss. "I think I'll throw you out of my home, after all," she said.

"You won't do that. You can't afford to do without me, literally speaking. But don't complain. The institute could have sent Lester Stetmueller when our lady tech got unexpectedly expecting."

"Lester Stetmueller? What is a Lester Stetmueller?"

"Lester Stetmueller is a Ph.D. on our psychic cataloging staff. Lester is five feet six, forty pounds underweight, has a chronic sniffle and poor circulation, talks through his nose when he isn't sniffling and through his ears when he is, complains about everything imaginable, hates his work vehemently, and his greatest ambition in life is to reap an edible harvest from the semidwarf Montague red plum tree in his backyard."

Judith grimaced. "Oh . . . poor Lester!"

"So, as you see, you have been blessed by fortune to have my inimitable presence in lieu of Lester's for the summer." He folded his arms and leaned forward, locking her eyes with his as securely as a nail into wood. "Still going to throw me out?"

She shrugged baitingly. "I might have to. Poor Lester needs a change."

"The last time I offered poor Lester a vacation or a field assignment, he accused me of not being able to take on a challenge myself. Thus," he tipped her chin upward, "thou art my challenge."

Judith felt suddenly self-conscious of her ragged, wet, muddy appearance, as his eyes swept her face in intimate scrutiny. "Jason," she said evasively, "I never know for sure when you're complimenting me."

His fingers brushed her cheekbone, then trailed along her jawbone to warm the tender area under her ear. Shocks of wild desire made her pulse roar.

The moments went by, counted in heartbeats.

"Well," he said, "I guess you'll just have to get to know me better."

The third Friday of the month was always a busy day at The Calico Patch, and Judith had to ask Jason to forestall testing until next week. Friday was the day when the month's products were shipped out to their various destinations. Judith's list of customers ranged from specialty shops to cosmetic outlets, health food co-ops, nurseries, and individuals who had bothered to contact her personally. Judith's reputation of dependability and flexibility had earned her a long roster of dedicated customers to whom she was completely loyal. Her heart had been warmed by the hordes of flowers and cards she had received from her clientele, many assuring her that they would be waiting for her to get well and return to business, that she need not fear losing them to other suppliers. She actually had lost a few customers who couldn't wait, but thanks to Peter's keeping the greenhouse plants growing and harvested, she was able to swing back into operation relatively soon after leaving the hospital.

Hiring a nurse to live-in and care for her mother had put still another financial strain on Judith, and Judith's mother had very few assets. The money the McNair Institute was offering would almost erase their debts, and now that she had admitted her love for Jason, Judith felt her resentment about the money fading away.

And suddenly the weeks ahead looked rosier, too. She delighted in waking up in Jason's arms each morning, found herself humming for no reason, and she was unaware that her great desire for privacy and solitude was waning in Jason's light.

In the middle of Friday afternoon, Peter finally goaded Judith into pausing for lunch. The two of them made tofu and watercress sandwiches and egg-drop soup while Jason loaded the crates of young plants and packaged seeds on Peter's father's pickup truck.

"You know," Jason commented as he sat at the table, "this vegetarian eating isn't all bad, if you know how to prepare it."

"That's right, it isn't," Judith said as she poured iced mint tea for everyone. "And I'm not going to thank you because I'm not sure that was a compliment."

Hastily Jason slipped out of the chair and dropped to one knee, catching Judith's hand in both of his. "Ah, madame, thou art the chef of chefs, the *cuisinière* of meatless meals, the *cordon bleu* of greenery—"

"Must I listen to this?" Judith protested, one hand on her hip, the other suffering noisy smooches from Jason while Peter rocked with giggles. Peter's laughter was almost as funny as Jason's carryings-on. The boy's mouth was stuffed with parts of one of four sandwiches he had reserved for himself, and he couldn't seem to decide if he wanted to stop eating long enough to laugh, or vice versa.

Jason continued to hold her hand in a firm grasp. "Sit down and eat with us. Your soup is cooling off."

Forcing herself to realize the sense of his words, Judith joined them. "Hyper, I guess. I'm always like this on Fridays."

"Don't worry. Everything's loaded on the truck. Nice to have a man around, isn't it?"

Judith shot him a quick warning glance and added, "I've always had a man around, right, Peter?"

"Yeah, sure. It only takes me four times as long to load the truck."

"We're still a good team. The job always gets done."

She hoped the subject would change before they got too deeply into it, before feelings got hurt, but she had underestimated the bond that Peter and Jason had cultivated between themselves.

"Peter's just a punk and he knows it," Jason teased.

"From the mouths of gorillas," Peter retaliated with a laugh.

Well, Judith thought, *better to let them get out of it on their own. Men! What pains they can be sometimes!*

With a grin she started eating with healthy slowness. Peter, however, was already on the second half of his second sandwich, despite all Judith's admonitions about eating too fast, and Jason had made at least two trips to the refrigerator for more iced tea and cheese. How men could eat.

At once Jason glanced at his watch. "Hm," he grunted, "Vic should be here anytime."

"What?" Judith looked up, her grin clattering to the floor. "Who?"

"My assistant. Vic. Ought to be arriving anytime now. I'm going to start organizing my notes on you and having them processed, so Vic will be spending a few days here every week or so."

"But . . . this is my busiest day," she protested. "I don't have time to spend with you and your assistant!"

"Don't worry about it. Vic and I have never had any trouble keeping each other occupied. Since you had the premonition about the ambulance, as well as the other visions you've told me about, we'll have plenty of data to coordinate. Vic's also bringing along some more tests that I want to specialize to your pattern."

"I wasn't aware I had a 'pattern.' "

With sly evasiveness, he smiled and said, "We all do." He masked any other questions with a heavy concentration on his meal.

Judith let the issue drop, but remained faintly disturbed

by the sudden change in arrangements. At least he could have informed her earlier about this new guest. He must have known for hours.

Well, maybe having another man around wouldn't be so bad, now that she was used to Jason's company.

There wasn't much time to concentrate on the change. Judith had her hands full finishing packing the crates of herb cosmetics, candles, culinary herb packets, and other various products of her trade, then carefully labeling each for efficient UPS shipment. By three o'clock, she was almost finished. Sam Viguera would be showing up any minute to drive them to the UPS office and help unload; Sam was the only human on earth who understood that pathetic pickup truck. Peter swore he would conquer it someday, though Judith had long ago given up, and even Jason's attempts at driving it had resulted in ungodly protests from the transmission. So, without fail, Sam appeared every Friday to coax the hunk of rubbish to make the drive. Judith had offered to pay half the price of a used truck in better condition, but Sam hadn't wanted to "hurt the old crate's feelings." He had always promised the truck that he would drive it until it just plain died, and then he would place it in an honored spot behind his barn with a brass plaque denoting its month and year of demise. So far, the stubborn old tank hadn't let them down more than twice in years.

Judith wiped the back of her hand across her forehead as she supervised the loading of the last few crates. Her arms were caked with dust and her face smudged with soil, but that was normal. She had tied her hair back into a sloppy ponytail to get it out of the way. Glancing at her hand, she noted without interest that she had probably just left a lovely black streak across her forehead. On Fridays, though, she never had time to care about her looks.

Oh, well, there would be time later for a long bath,

106

complete with all her favorite homemade oils, and bubbles too.

"Here comes my dad, Judith," Peter called from the greenhouse, pointing toward the meadow where a tiny figure was slowly closing the distance. Sam Viguera's stocky form was skirted in waist-high meadow grass and wild flowers, and he waved at them leisurely after relighting his Sherlock Holmes pipe. That pipe was as perpetual with Sam as the rag hanging out of Peter's back pocket.

A swish of nostalgia ran over Judith, reminding her how much she liked the pleasant normality of her lifestyle, the familiar things and people in it. Now that Jason had shown her that a man could be strong and kind and loving without being fickle, she was sure she had everything in the world a young woman could want.

Sam Viguera hadn't even made it halfway across the meadow when the buzzing of a car eased out of the midday landscape, and a flame-red BMW skimmed into view.

"Oh, good," Jason said. "Vic finally made it. I wanted you to at least say hello before you had to leave."

The car pulled into Judith's front yard and Jason ran to meet it as Judith wiped filthy hands on even filthier jeans and followed him.

The sight stopped her short as she came around the edge of the cabin. Jason was standing at the driver's side of the car grasping both hands of what was certainly no male assistant.

The young woman was enviably petite, with hair like ebony, about two inches below shoulder-length, carefully curled into a tumble of sun-catching waves. She was meticulously groomed, wearing a white blouse with a delicate ruffled collar and sleeves; the blouse was captured into the waistband of a straight business skirt that followed her round buttocks down to where shapely legs took over.

Oh, no, Judith thought, *I look like a trail horse next to*

107

her! Maybe they wouldn't notice if she dashed into town for a complete salon treatment and a new wardrobe—

"Judith, come here and meet my assistant," Jason beckoned to her.

Too late. Make the best of it.

"Sure, why not . . ." she mumbled, and dug up a smile.

"Judith Longfellow," Jason began as she drew closer, "this is Victoria Phillips, my tech assistant."

"Miss Longfellow," Victoria Phillips greeted melodically.

"Hi," Judith returned. *Oh, great. A voice like a nightingale besides. I always wanted to have someone around like her.*

"Did you bring everything?" Jason asked, glancing into the backseat.

"Of course." Victoria put even weight on both heels and smiled coquettishly at him.

"I knew I could count on you." He gestured Judith's way. "She's a live one. We have our work cut out for us."

"Oh? You don't mean to say that we have a genuine psychic here." Was she kidding?

"I do mean to say it. At least, I have reason to suspect so." Jason ran a hand down Victoria's arm with a familiarity that Judith did not fail to notice.

"Judith has work to do," Jason said, rescuing Judith from having to make small talk. She was sure she couldn't utter an intelligible sound. Psychic, and now dumbstruck. What next? "Let's get this paraphernalia inside and I'll get you settled. Don't worry about us, Judith," he added as he led "Vic" into the cabin. "We'll be fine by ourselves."

"Funny," she grumbled when they were gone, "but I don't doubt it."

As she stood there with her eyes fixed on the door of the cabin, she couldn't help wondering why her bothersome ability to foresee trouble hadn't prepared her for "Vic."

CHAPTER TEN

By the time Peter and Sam Viguera were waving good-bye to Judith as she stood before the cabin in the pickup's choking exhaust, it was already almost dark.

As grimy and exhausted as she was, she had done everything possible to stall their return, including goading Sam into letting her treat them to dinner in town.

However, now that she stood in the evening's coolness outside the home that somehow didn't seem very welcoming, she realized that she had made a mistake. If Jason had any romantic interest in Victoria Phillips, she had given them an ideal opportunity to revive it. Her absence had no doubt tilled ground for comparison between her grimy self and the pristine Ms. Phillips, allowing Jason to come to his own conclusions.

Judith didn't even want to go inside now and let herself be foiled against Victoria's perfect appearance. Maybe she could spend the night in the greenhouse. Take a bath in the river. Greet them in the morning with wild flowers plaited in her medieval braids, her body clad only in vines of blossoming flora, perfumed with the scent of old roses.
. . .

Sighing, she brushed back the limp straggles of hair that had wriggled free of the ponytail, which now had lost its brushed luster and gone dull with the day's work.

"Bleh," she editorialized. "I am a walking yuk."

A loud banging of the screen door drew her attention.

Cashel's furry red face was entreating her to come in, and after a pause he decided a long whine would bring her to him.

"Coming, you traitor," she muttered, and squared her shoulders to go inside.

"Hello there," Jason raised his head as she walked in. He and Victoria were lounging on the floor amid assorted papers and books. Jason was stretched out comfortably, his legs crossed and his head back on a huge muslin pillow. Victoria had changed into a caftan and was nestled on the sheepskin rug with a mug of coffee, only inches from Jason. In fact, they were reading the same pamphlet. "We heard you drive up," Jason said. "What took you so long to come in?"

"I was enjoying the fresh air," she said, forcing a casual smile. "Since you weren't alone, I didn't bother to hurry back." She could only hope her feigned aplomb would disguise the truth. "I hope you helped yourself to dinner."

"We did. Vic is an excellent cook and had no trouble whipping up a good breakfast for dinner. We had eggs, pancakes, the works."

"It seemed a little bland without bacon or sausage, though," Victoria was compelled to add.

"Not if you ask the pig," Judith retorted with a sugary smile. "Well, if you'll excuse me, I'll tidy up. It's been a long day."

"I guess running your own business isn't easy," Victoria said. "Jason tells me you're a regular workhorse."

Bristling, Judith managed to keep her smile going until she ducked into the hallway, where she snarled at Cashel for lack of something to throw. Undaunted, Cashel followed her eagerly, but she slammed the bathroom door in his face, and was sorry for it.

A workhorse. She had given him every ounce of womanhood she had to give, and he described her as a workhorse. Suddenly she felt like a casual acquaintance instead

110

of the woman whose bed Jason had so ardently shared. She wondered if, with Victoria's arrival, she was being shunted back to her original position as subject of a sober investigation.

As she soaked in the steaming tub of herb-scented water, her tension ebbed and her hostility began to rise away in the steam. "Paranoid," she told herself. "I'm putting an honorable man in the same category with my father and that arrogant Don Juan I almost married. Jason loves me," she said with resolve, "he doesn't care if I was a little gritty today. Hasn't he praised my looks enough times for me to have a little confidence? I'm being unfair to him."

Her worries dissolved one by one as she warmly recalled the nights of passion they had shared and the quiet times of lying in his protective embrace as he caressed her hair and savored every inch of her soft creamy skin. By the time she rinsed herself with cool water Judith was convinced that Victoria was no threat to her. After all, Victoria was an assistant, a professional colleague, someone Jason had probably worked with so long that the novelty of her doll-like loveliness had worn off.

Judith splashed herself with after-bath cologne and suddenly felt vibrant and competitive. No one was going to come between her and Jason! She was determined to have the sweet rewards of this romantic victory, this encounter with a man's true emotions. And she wouldn't let another woman upstage her in her own element. If Jason hadn't already formed an attachment to Victoria, Judith wouldn't allow it to begin here!

She dug through her closet until she found the white silk lounging pajama her mother had given her for her twenty-fourth birthday; it was old but almost completely unused. In fact, it still had the original creases along the sleeves and legs where it had been folded for so long. It was heavily scented with sachet, a flowery scent that hadn't faded much despite years of confinement in a lin-

111

gerie box. It was a tad snug, but Judith subconsciously wanted it that way, though she wouldn't have admitted it even to herself. She stood before her mirror and preened at the sparkling lady in white silk, all oiled and perfumed to smooth perfection, her long hair still moist at the neck, curled just enough to be naturally alluring. She dabbed on enough lip gloss to moisten her towel-dried lips, then braved the frontier she had prepared herself for.

But the cabin was empty.

Confused, she went to each window and peeked outside, but no one was in sight. She was dreadfully denying the temptation to check the loft when she found a note on the kitchen counter. It was from Jason.

> Got bored with your brain and decided to take a walk to show Vic the evening countryside. Know you're tired, so don't wait up for us. Sleep well.

> Jace

Not "Love, Jace." Just "Jace."

She tried not to notice that detail, but it seemed to jump out at her.

Her shoulders sagged. Loneliness set in anew.

Feeling quite like an unripened fruit that had been knocked uselessly to the cold wet ground, she rubbed the silky material of the lounging pajamas around her arms with icy hands, turned, and retired to bed. There seemed to be no other choice.

She awakened to two unsavory sensations: the lilt of Victoria's laughter cutting through the morning peace, and the realization that Jason had not come to her bed last night.

The realization hit her like a dash of cold water and she sat up abruptly.

112

Why was last night different from the past nights of contentment and love making?

As she dressed quickly in a denim jump suit and raked a brush through her hair, only one answer to that question would come to her mind.

Had he actually spent the night with Victoria?

"Morning."

Not "Morning, darling." Not "Morning, love." Not even "Morning, Judith."

Jason planted a fresh cup of coffee in Victoria's small white hand, magnifying for Judith the calluses on her own palms and the workaday nails that never quite shook free the minute specks from underneath. Jason had on only a pair of jeans. Victoria had on only a nightgown. No robe. Just a rather revealing lacy nightgown. A pink revealing lacy nightgown. A pink *satin* revealing lacy nightgown.

Judith stifled a groan of defeat. Victoria's hair looked perfect already. One could hardly tell she had slept on it—if she had.

"Want some coffee?" Jason offered.

"Always," Judith answered. "So," she began, as she dished out some dog food for Cashel, "did you accomplish much last night?" Suddenly she hoped she hadn't put too much emphasis on the wrong words.

"I'll say," Jason said. "Vic is going back to Philadelphia with a full load of work to do. We've arranged all my data on you and your recorded visions for computer cataloging, then Vic will run your program and see if we can't correlate some similar cases. Fascinating, right?"

"Riveting."

"I'm sure you don't need to confuse yourself," Victoria said, "with all our scientific jargon. Our investigations are designed to be somewhat simplistic at first, for the sake of our subjects."

Huge black eyes widened innocently.

113

"Don't worry about me," Judith said, "I'm not confused. After all, we college girls are used to a little mellow contemplation from time to time."

Victoria laughed for a long time, too long for sincerity. "When I got my degree, the going joke was that college women were expressly trained to provide suitable intelligent conversation for marriage to college men. Isn't that a riot?"

A regular tumult, Judith thought. *How witty thou art.*

"What did you get your degree in, Miss Longfellow?"

Trapped.

"Well . . . I didn't finish my degree work, though I studied horticulture." She didn't clarify that she had only gone to college for one year. Victoria didn't need to know that. "I grabbed a business opportunity when it popped up and got immersed in it. Luckily," she added firmly, "it paid off."

Victoria nodded socially and gestured to Jason. "Dr. McNair and I lived in the same dorm at Penn State. We've been working together in psychology just forever. Not including the three years Jason was doing research in England, of course."

Then Judith looked up sharply. "You lived in England for three years?"

"Of course," Jason said smoothly. "Didn't I tell you that?"

"Must have slipped your mind," she answered in bold tones. How could he have missed telling her something so integral to his personhood? Why did she feel more and more like a stranger with every breath?

"If you have no objections, Judith, Vic and I are going to take a ride out to Bakerville. My sister lives there with her husband and their little girl. It's only a forty-five-minute drive, and I'd like the opportunity to visit them. Think you can keep busy without us around to occupy you?" He started to say something else, but was choked by a sudden cough. "Excuse me. I feel a slight cold on the way."

"You'll have to take care of yourself," Victoria warned. "We can pick something up for you at a drugstore in Bakerville." She looked at Judith patronizingly. "We can't have him coming down with pneumonia, can we?"

"Actually," Judith explained, "one doesn't get pneumonia from a simple chest cold."

"One can if one has had pneumonia before," Victoria went on.

"Did one have it before?"

"Yes, one had it big," Jason droned. "Thought I was going to flatten out and die."

"I was hovering over this poor baby for weeks," Victoria added. "Wasn't I, dear?"

He nodded. "You were, I admit. Vic, why don't you get dressed and I'll call Carolyn."

"I won't be long." With a smile, Victoria retired to the bathroom.

"You don't mind our leaving, do you?" Jason asked, unable to keep from chasing it with a stifled cough.

"Of course not."

"I'm anxious to see my sister and her family. Dori is only a year and a half old, and every time I see her it's like seeing a whole new person, she grows so fast."

"Jason?"

"Yes?"

She hesitated, but was sure she had to continue. "Why didn't you come to bed last night?" Carefully, without emphasis, she added, "With me, I mean."

He paused, a hesitation she noticed. "We got back from our walk quite late, but my mind was still working. I settled down on the hammock to read an article, and fell asleep. I felt a bit silly when I woke up there. Had a backache, too. I guess I'm too tall to sleep all night on a hammock." He leaned over and pecked her cheek, turned

115

away to cough, then bit into a kiwi fruit he had discovered in the refrigerator.

Sniffles had set in and Jason's eyes were red by the time he had put a shirt on, changed into a sleek pair of tan slacks, and called Victoria to hurry.

"I'll give you something for that cold if you're no better by the time you get back," Judith said, preoccupied by doubts.

"Country cures, eh?"

"Don't laugh. Every medicine started as a natural element, and almost all of them started as country remedies."

"I shall submit to your care, Dr. Longfellow." He sneezed then and tried to keep from coughing during his phone call to his sister.

Judith felt intensely dissatisfied with his answer about not coming to bed with her. Had he hesitated as long as it seemed to her? Had he been thinking up an excuse? Even if he hadn't spent the night with Victoria, had he deliberately *not* wanted Victoria to know that he and Judith had become lovers?

Why not?

She shivered. There seemed to be no way to discover the truth. She had to stand there and watch Jason drive away with Victoria, and stare likewise into the face of the long day during which she would be filled with apprehension.

Was it simply a lack of security? A lack of confidence in herself as a woman? In her ability to make a man love her and her alone? Or had he really been acting more distant since Victoria came? Was he protecting Judith's reputation—or his own?

Her hands trembled all day. She felt cheapened by Jason's subtle changes since the arrival of his "assistant," and was becoming more and more certain that there was sexuality humming in the currents between Jason and Victoria.

Yet, she was unable to shake memories of his gentle-

116

ness, the delicate fire of his tongue against her flesh, the whispers of secrets only true lovers could share. How could she doubt the man whose caresses had freed her from her fears of all men?

That must be it . . . her fears were making her hypersensitive. She tried hard to think back, to recall details of Jason's reactions to Victoria, and to herself since Victoria showed up. Had it all been imagination, or had Victoria's eyes carried a knowing flicker when she looked at Jason?

Maybe. . . .

Maybe not.

But . . . maybe.

She could only hope that things would return to what they had been before Victoria's arrival.

She hoped it very, very much.

Judith was making soaps that evening. Though preoccupied with Jason's peculiar behavior, she felt an intense need to be independent, to feel satisfied with her own skills, and to feel as though she could depend on her own emotional stability.

Still, her hands shook as she stirred the melting shavings of castile and glycerin soaps in three iron pots. As the soaps dissolved, she added essential oils of violet and rose in one pot, sandalwood and cinnamon in the second, and walnut and rum extracts in the third. The thick aromas mixed to drift through the cabin and warm the atmosphere, merging with the soft guitar music from Judith's stereo. She ground almonds in a mortar and pestle until they were crushed thoroughly, then sprinkled them into the third pot to create a soothing scrub for her customers. Her walnut-almond-rum scrub was one of the most popular items from The Calico Patch.

When the dissolving process was complete, the liquid was poured into various molds, some leaf-shaped, some with imprints that would show up on the hardened soap,

117

and some into shaving mugs. The whole process was very tranquilizing, something Judith needed badly right now.

She put the soaps aside to harden, then went about cutting up clumps of sea sponges to be sold with the soaps as facial care items. Even if she hadn't been an herbalist, she knew she would prefer the sea sponges to ordinary man-made sponges, so she understood her customers' desire for them. She ordered them by tens from a tiny shell shop in Cocoa Beach, Florida.

As a matter of fact, her whole occupation was damn satisfying, and fun, too. So why did she feel so dependent on Jason's next move?

All her efforts at calming herself went flying out the window in a draft of soapy perfume when she heard the car roar into the vicinity and grind to a stop outside the cabin.

Although she really was busy, her hands involuntarily moved faster as she heard Jason's cough and Victoria's twittering voice outside.

They greeted her as they came in, but any response she might have given was lost as she noticed Victoria carrying a tiny red-haired girl, hardly more than a baby.

"Judith, I'm sorry we took so long," Jason said, his voice gravelly from a sore throat. His eyes were glassy and his face flushed, obviously because his cold had continued to get worse instead of better. "And I owe you another apology. This is Dori, my niece. I wasn't planning to drop all of this on you, but my sister's husband fell off a ladder and broke his leg this afternoon, and I offered to watch Dori for a day or so to free Carolyn. I hope you understand."

Judith couldn't resist the request that came up in his chestnut eyes as sparkles of hope. "Of course, I understand," she said, hurrying to take the child from Victoria. The move was a good one. "It's no problem, Jason. I love children, and I don't see many of them since Peter's little brothers started going to school. She can stay as long as needed."

He looked relieved and flexed back into the overstuffed chair. "I knew I could count on you." He started to say more, but was thrown into a violent series of sneezes. His eyes watered as he spoke through a Kleenex. "I hesitated to bring her because I don't want to give her my cold. But Carolyn was so distraught I had to offer."

"Jason is a natural humanitarian," Victoria said. "He's a wonderful brother to Carolyn, and like a second daddy to Dori. Isn't she sweet?"

"She's beautiful," Judith acknowledged, determined to be cordial as she held the small child and studied the pixieish face.

"She's a very independent baby," Victoria warned. "Why, before you know it she'll be wandering off, exploring the territory. You'll have to be careful that she doesn't pop any of your plants into her mouth. We wouldn't want to poison her accidentally, would we?" She pursed her lips into something that could only dubiously be described as a smile, and moved provocatively to Jason's side. "I have your prescription right here in my bag. I'll make sure you take it regularly through tomorrow, but after I leave, you'll be on your own."

Judith stifled a desire to draw attention to herself with a whistle.

"Don't worry," Jason said. "I promise to take the whole prescription religiously. Pneumonia is no fun, and I don't intend to court trouble."

"Well, in that case," Victoria said musically, "I won't worry. But don't be surprised if you get a phone call during the week. It'll be me checking on you." She pressed an intimate hand across his forehead. "You do have a fever. Maybe I should stay an extra day or two."

Clumsily Judith sprung in. "His fever will be gone by

119

tomorrow, Victoria. I have a few tricks up my sleeve in the country medicine department."

Victoria turned to her, perfect brows launched in tall arches. "Oh? I'll be interested to watch and see how well you do. You're so talented, Miss Longfellow." She excused herself, saying it was time for her bath. In a last-ditch effort at cordiality, Judith offered her an herbal bath oil.

"Oh, I couldn't," Victoria demurred.

"I insist. I have plenty of it."

Victoria's white hand fluttered in declination. "Thank you anyway, but I never use anything but water and lanolin on my skin. After all," she laughed, "my complexion goes all the way down my body." With flair, she exited.

Cashel was dancing at Judith's feet, nudging her in an effort to get at Dori, and the little girl reached down at the dog's huge nose. Cashel wrapped a long pink tongue around the tiny hand.

"Okay, okay." Judith put the little redhead down on the sheepskin rug, and Cashel immediately plunked his big self down beside her, rolling into the child's lap and begging for a cuddle. Dori dug her stubby baby fingers into the copper coat of the setter and laughed, showing a set of sparse new teeth and beaming up at Judith.

"They look adorable," Jason observed, "both redheads and all." He was plainly becoming more miserable by the minute, and he let his head fall back. "My head feels like a balloon and my chest feels like a gravel pit."

"I'll make you some goldenseal tea and something for your throat." Judith tried to keep her tone from sounding too plastic, but it was a struggle.

"Don't I get a kiss first?"

"What?"

He raised his head. "You mean you've forgotten already?" His eyes washed over her like liquid, sultry and provocative despite the glassiness brought on by his cold. What was his game and why did she feel like a pawn?

"Have you eaten dinner yet?"

"Is that a change of subject?" He pushed himself out of the chair and wearily crossed the room, pausing to tousle Dori's soft red topknot before reaching Judith. He coiled his arms around her and drew her close to his fever-warmed body, laying his head down on her shoulder and nuzzling the soft skin under her ear. His lips found their way down her collarbone, sending shots of electricity through her limbs.

Paralyzed with tension and arousal, Judith lost all conscious ability to make the decision of whether to push him away or submit as her body urged her to with its tremors of response. Surges of desire drove up her legs like electricity, but she was curiously relieved when Jason loosened his tight hold and moaned, "Oh, God, I feel like death itself." He leaned on her heavily, and only then did she realize how sick he was.

"Lie down on the couch," she suggested. "I'll take care of you right away."

"I'll let you. Anything would be an improvement." He coughed again, a wheezy cough from deep in his chest. In a vain effort to get comfortable, he unbuckled his belt and drew it out of the belt loops, then pulled the tails of his shirt free of his pants.

"Here," Judith said, handing him a capsule. "Time-released vitamin C. It's the best thing for you."

While he was resting, Judith prepared the goldenseal tea, not mentioning to him the inherent bitter tase of it, and warmed a saucepan of honey, comfrey root, and menthol for his cough.

When the tea was fully brewed, she strained a cupful into a mug and hoped his tastebuds were numb. "Here you go," she said, delivering it to him. "Goldenseal tea. You'll have to down at least two cups."

121

"You're a wonderful nurse," he said, running one hand from her waist to the back of her thigh. Judith couldn't help but notice that such a move would have gone lacking if Victoria had been present. He took a cautious sip of the tea, then grimaced. "That's awful!"

"I know," Judith said sympathetically, "I hate it, too. But it's excellent for you."

"I have to put down two cups of this stuff?"

"You do indeed. I have to cure you, remember? If I don't, I lose face with Victoria."

He chuckled. "Women. Your opinions of each other positively rule your lives."

Coolly she noted, "I'm glad to know you think of me as so typical."

His eyes swept electrically along the contours of her breasts, down the long waistline to roam indecently around her hips. "You're anything but typical, Judith," he remarked with a trace of ragged hunger forcing up through his raw throat. He almost spilled his tea as a cough racked his body then with a regretful groan he said, "I think I'll sleep out here tonight. I don't want to make you uncomfortable with my tossing if this cold keeps me awake. You won't mind, will you?" The question came in tones that made it a statement, a finality he had already decided upon. It was clear she had no say in the matter.

A terrible clutch of fear caught her throat tight. Perhaps she hadn't been imagining things at all . . . perhaps it was wholly true that he didn't want Victoria to know of the sexual intimacy that had blossomed between him and Judith.

Judith was becoming more and more afraid to know the reason why.

She spent the next several hours in the coolness of the warehouse, puttering with everything and anything that looked like it needed doing. Mostly she was shifting back

122

and forth between troublesome suspicions and reassuring memories of times alone with Jason. The fire was real, there was no doubt of that. Her passion for him had flowered as surely as her harvest into a lush bouquet of love. But her sixth sense was buzzing loudly, her fear and distrust of the male ego's power over the male sense of devotion.

Dori was asleep in a makeshift sleeping bag on the sheepskin rug with Cashel spread out beside her, Jason had fallen asleep on the couch, and Victoria was in the loft; at least that had been the situation when Judith first came to the greenhouse, but she could easily imagine Victoria floating down from the loft to further drift around Jason. Judith was unable to clearly delineate Jason's feelings for Victoria, except that he definitely liked having his assistant around. Any other, more intense feelings were disguised. Victoria's feelings toward Jason, though . . . well, those had gone uncamouflaged. Victoria had drawn no curtains around her designs on Jason McNair. Were they fruitless essays that had gone on for time untold, or could it be that Victoria was guarding a claim she had already staked? Was her smugness a result of the knowledge that she, in the end, would win out?

Judith shook her head in confusion. She had been out of social circulation too long to know if she was interpreting other people's signals correctly. If that was so . . . how could she be certain of Jason's true, deep, inner feelings toward her?

The thought made her unsatisfied and frustrated with the odds and ends of work she was doing, so she gave it up and left the greenhouse.

The moon rested between the black mountains like a pearl shining between the breasts of a reclining woman, and the Pennsylvania night panorama stretched out before her like a dark sea. She longed to sail it, so she indulged herself with a long walk down by the river.

The willows and oaks waved complacently against an opaque sky, and even in the dimness of night the countryside welcomed her as an old friend might. There was a chill in the air, though, and Judith looked suspiciously at a pall of clouds that was loping slowly in from the western horizon. Yes, there would be rain tonight, probably light rain, enough to loosen the soil for a preliminary tilling tomorrow. Maybe she could prepare the ground well enough this week to start the first cycle of outdoor planting next week.

These thoughts distracted her sufficiently until the first droplets of misty rain whispered across the meadow. Her long thick hair was unbound and provided some protection, so Judith wasn't ready to head home yet.

The rain began as a soft moist breath and drifted into a mild spritz of raindrops that dampened Judith's clothing and made a light fog rise over the river, but it didn't seem to be thinking about turning into a torrent, or even a noticeable shower, so she continued her walk. Eventually it didn't seem so chilly, and she followed the river farther down toward the covered bridge, never expecting what the rain would trigger.

The old covered bridge was a landmark in the area, and had recently been renovated for safe travel and as a historical monument by the county government. The move had strengthened Judith's estimation of her fellow Pennsylvanians, because the bridge was extraneous since the expressway had rerouted most of the traffic to more scenic areas with towns and restaurants to accomodate travelers. But they hadn't condemned the old relic; in fact they'd bothered to rebuild it. So Judith had bothered to send a thank-you note to the county board of trustees for using her tax money aesthetically.

Now, as she stood under the protection of the wooden canopy, she leaned on the rail and watched the water rush toward the rapids that ran near Bakerville, where Jason said his sister lived. The river eventually became wide and deep, an industrial tool for the miners, but here it was still a mellow twenty-five feet across, still just a trickle on a postcard. Judith was thinking about the river when the water beneath her seemed to fog unaccountably. The fog rose and engulfed her, and only then did she realize with coldness that the fog was not on the river; it was in her mind.

She tried to shake it away, but the vision was too strong this time.

Her heart leaped when Jason's face came into focus. His eyes were closed, his face wet, his dark hair plastered down by driving rain. His face was heavy with a placid expression, an expression of ultimate peace, of such concord that Judith caught her breath in fear of rupturing it.

In her vision it was raining furiously, with lightning flickering silently behind her imagination.

She was helpless to do anything but watch as the reel played out in her mind.

Jason's rain-drenched face, his arms, a dark head against his chest—

Judith's heart skipped a beat.

Jason was holding a woman in his arms. A woman with long dark hair, small and delicate stature, cleaving as tightly to Jason as he was holding her against him.

Tears mixed with the mist on Judith's cheeks as she recognized Victoria in Jason's arms, and noted again the expression of complete fulfillment on his face. There was no chance of mistake, no matter how much she wanted it not to be true. She remembered hopelessly that her psychic mind had never lied to her. Every vision had come relentlessly to be, without fail, without error, and without change.

She fought to hang on to the vision, to see what circumstances would make Jason stand in the rain with Victoria in a fervent embrace, his face a canvas of tranquility.

Yet her mind betrayed her.

The image began to powder.

Tears ran down Judith's cheeks, washing from her mind's eye the cruel sight that confirmed her worst fears. As the image drew dim and churned to become once again the river under the bridge, she felt her heart squeeze in a new kind of agony in knowing that no extension of the vision could change that which was inevitable.

She was deeply in love with a man she was destined, irrevocably, to lose.

CHAPTER ELEVEN

After a time, a few hours in the misty night, Judith's desperate sobs ran dry and a dull inertia overtook her senses. At first she blamed Jason, cried out a mindless roster of horrid names and accusations. Then she blamed Victoria for interrupting the wonder of their passionate togetherness. Then she blamed herself. She had encouraged him to use her, with her silence, with her failure to tell him how she felt about men, and finally with her body's passionate response to his sensuous availability.

Had it been only that? Only that Jason was there? Available? That he was an intrepid example of manliness whose electrifying presence she had responded to out of some kind of second adolescence, some revived ignorance of men?

No matter how she tried to analyze it, from whatever angle she tried to approach it, the truth always surfaced unaltered. She was going to lose Jason. She knew it now as totally irreversible. Perhaps even Jason didn't know it yet. Victoria seemed to know, though. Her whole attitude suggested the awful reality that Judith's clairvoyance had shown her.

Her mind was trying to protect her. Her psychic, healing brain sensed danger and was warning her.

Very well, she would take the warning.

She would have to let go.

She thought about putting up a good fight for her man,

but always the truth came crashing down upon her: he was not, would not be, her man. Not now, or ever. He would stand in a romantic rainstorm, his arms wrapped possessively around Victoria, his face limned in ultimate happiness as he realized whom he really loved.

She felt empty, hollow, as she moved mindlessly back to the cabin. She was glad it was night. She had a few long hours alone before she had to begin being really, totally, alone.

One thing was sure. The physical relationship between herself and Jason would have to come to an abrupt halt.

Jason would wonder why, but it would have to stop. Judith could not allow herself to be further used, especially now that there would be nothing but agony in it for her. A quiver ran down her spine. She feared his reaction and his confusion, but this was one vision she could not explain to him, as she had the others. He wouldn't know about this, she resolved. She would resist him no matter how much it hurt—and it would hurt so terribly much—and she would make him think she was rejecting him for her own reasons, not because she knew his future, the future that would take him to another woman's arms.

And she would do it gracefully. He would never know.

Much to Jason's surprise and Victoria's masked chagrin, his fever was gone by morning and his cough was reduced to a sandpapery tenderness in his throat. He also wasn't sneezing anymore, much to his relief, and allowed himself a session of play with Dori. As much as she wanted to remain aloof and unattached, the squeeze of love was too tight on Judith's heart as she gazed at Jason, the pinch of misery too close when she recalled the destiny she knew to be inevitable.

Forlornly she went about her business, made their breakfast, then left them alone. She was heedless of Jason's concerned gaze as it followed her, but she could almost sense the shrugging off of his responsibility for her well-being as he concentrated on Victoria's imminent departure and on Dori's presence. Victoria would leave for now, but, Judith knew, she would never really be gone. Her presence would be there in Jason's presence, forever reminding Judith of the brutal destiny that she and Jason would not share.

Oh, damn her psychic mind! Wouldn't it have been better to go on ignorantly loving Jason, accepting the fire of his hands on her body, the quenching rising of her own body against his, to know at least the motions of love if not the inner totality of lovers? Wouldn't it have been kinder for her mind to leave her unaware of the inevitable? At least then the next endless weeks would be spent in delirious stupidity on her part, and she would have loved him without the agony of *knowing* she would lose him. Now she would have to live through the weeks with that bitter knowledge, and somehow she would have to hide from him the reasons for her rejection of him.

That afternoon, Victoria drove away with all the data on Judith that she was to correlate, leaving behind fertile ground for Judith's anxieties to take root.

On Monday, Jason's sister called to have Dori returned, and Jason invited Judith to make the drive with him. Since it was her least busy day of the month, and since she saw an opportunity to avoid being conspicuously alone with Jason, she accepted.

Carolyn McNair-White lived in the small rural settlement of Bakerville, where seventy percent of the work force were coal miners. Carolyn's husband, Brian, the one with the broken leg, was a senior foreman with the company that mined the Bakerville area, and Carolyn was a freelance writer who had enjoyed success with many articles and two textbooks. Apparently, like Jason, Carolyn was no intellectual slouch.

She was, as Judith came to know during lunch at their

cottage on stilts on the Bakerville cliffs, an especially warm and easygoing woman. She was about Judith's age, and Brian, a tall man who had passed on his red hair to his daughter, was about thirty. Brian was home already, his right leg encased in plaster from the knee down. His friendly face was pale, telling them that he was still in some pain, but he had no trouble participating in the conversation.

"Yeah, I'm a klutz by nature," he was saying. "That's why they had to take me out of the mine and make me a foreman. Now I yell a lot and push papers at the field office."

"They figured out that's all you were good for," Jason commented dryly. He and Brian shared a caustically jovial amity, Judith noticed early on. Words between them had been almost exclusively wry insults since they arrived.

After lunch, Brian turned to Jason and entreated, "Jace, how about a lift to the living room?"

"Do I look like a taxi to you?"

"Only a little around the headlights."

"That's my lot in life," Jason admitted. "Destined forever to aid helpless incompetents."

"Thanks," Judith said.

"Ditto," Brian added as Jason hoisted him up and wrapped an arm around him, drawing Brian's arm around his neck.

"Wouldn't a wheelchair be more sensible?"

"I refuse to sit in a wheelchair, McNair. It would make my pride sore." He tried to put weight on his walking cast, but the leg wasn't willing yet and he fell against Jason.

"You okay?" Jason asked him.

"Do I look okay? Sometimes I question your powers of observation."

"Sometimes I question my sister's."

When they were gone, Carolyn and Judith cleaned up the lunch dishes and had a chance to talk.

130

"I'm sorry about dumping Dori on you yesterday," Carolyn said, brushing back a wild lock of her hair, which was a shade or two darker than Jason's and tied up in a loose twist at the back of her head. "I was really a mess. I practically panicked when I saw that ladder start to slide. Usually I'm a rock, but I guess being pregnant makes me hypersensitive."

"Are you pregnant?" Judith asked as she wiped a serving plate.

"Four months. We didn't really want to have our second so soon after Dori, but I have a slight heart condition and my doctor recommended we finish up having our family before I'm thirty-five."

"How many children do you and Brian want?"

"We'd like three. So we decided to go for it, diapers and all."

A twinge of envy picked at Judith as she looked around the charming little house, with its photos of the happy young family, or Dori and her father with "Uncle Jace," who seemed to fit into the family scenes like a hand in a leather glove.

Carolyn noticed what had drawn Judith's attention. "He's wonderful to Dori."

Embarrassed, Judith saw that she couldn't put anything by Carolyn. She nodded. "I've noticed he's very fond of her."

Carolyn smiled a regretful smile. "Ever since Lesley died, Jason's been preoccupied with my family life. When Dori came along, it was as though he finally had a chance to watch a little girl grow up, like the baby he lost. Luckily for me, Brian and Jace get along great, so I don't have any friction to deal with. You know how possessive men can be." She laughed, and Judith did too, but inside, Judith was not laughing.

"I'd like to have children myself someday," she said,

131

unable to hold back the wistfulness, "but fate hasn't cast those cards in my direction yet."

"I hope you know what you're getting into. Dori's a real handful. She's not the type that clings to Mama's ankle, I can tell you that."

"I know," Judith said. "Twice we turned around and she was halfway across the meadow with my dog."

"She loves animals. Heaven knows where she got it. I don't have any affinity for critters at all. Sometimes I swear that child doesn't have a natural fear in her body. She's the most daring little squirt I've ever encountered. With the railroad tracks practically in our bathroom and the river right down the slope, we really have to keep an eye on her."

"Mission accomplished," Jason announced as he strode into the kitchen. "Now his royal highness would like some more coffee, please."

"Honestly, Jace, we'd better watch out we don't spoil him. By the time he gets that cast off, he'll be impossible to live with." The three of them laughed as Carolyn poured some coffee into a mug and fixed it with milk and sugar. "I have to go to the market, if no one minds my rudeness. Do you two have to hurry away, or can you stay for supper?"

"It's up to Judith. She has a business to run," Jason said. "As long as she's around, my duty is portable."

"What do you say, Judith?" Carolyn looked hopeful. "I could use some company."

Feeling an unusual need for another woman's company, Judith allowed herself to weaken. "I suppose there's no reason to rush to get back. I'd like to phone Peter, my helper, and tell him he can go home. He'd work all day if I didn't show up. He's still at a stage where he thinks working is fun."

"The blindness of adolescence," Jason commented.

"Good," Carolyn said cheerily. "Come on with me,

Judith. You can help me choose the right ingredients for a complete vegetarian meal. It'll be a real treat in this meat-and-potatoes household."

Somehow, being with Carolyn made Judith feel closer to Jason. Carolyn's steady stream of conversation was lightly intimate, and by the middle of the afternoon Judith felt she had known this unpretentious woman for years. Carolyn took an honest interest in Judith's unwanted clairvoyance, and it made Judith feel relaxed that Carolyn took the whole oddity as a matter of course. It made her feel like less of a freak and more of a victim.

"I sometimes wonder if studying me is going to be worthwhile for Jason's institute," she confided as they strolled the impersonal aisle of the local grocery store. "My visions have become less and less frequent lately."

"Jason says that's normal in injury-activated clairvoyance," Carolyn assured her. "Don't even worry about it. If Jason's investigating your case, I'm sure he feels you're worth the stipend."

He had other rewards, Judith thought, trying not to be resentful. *But that's over.*

"Want a dish of ice cream after we check out?"

"Hm?" Judith snapped out of her own thoughts. "Oh . . . sure, that would be nice."

Carolyn giggled. "I don't really have any cravings when I'm pregnant, but it's a terrific excuse to nibble!"

They loaded the grocery bags into Carolyn's station wagon and drove two blocks to a dumpy diner with lots of what Carolyn described as "character."

"They make their own ice cream in the back, and it makes store-bought ice cream taste like water. I always get the fudge ripple, but they have all kinds. I'll get us some coffee—you pour your own in this place. Then we can relax. It usually takes old Mrs. Langstrom awhile to get out here. Pick a table and get comfortable, then when I get back you can tell me what's bothering you."

133

Carolyn winked knowingly at Judith's appalled expression, and mellowed the surprise with a grin.

When Carolyn came to the table with two steaming mugs of thick coffee, Judith had prepared a dozen reassurances that nothing was bothering her at all and why ever would Carolyn suppose such a thing?

"Because even in this age of women's lib and ERA, I still think women have a sixth sense about each other's feelings," Carolyn explained as Judith felt her face flush slightly. "You don't strike me as a quiet person, yet you've been preoccupied and let me do all the talking."

Stammering, Judith argued, "It's just that I've had a busy month and I'm trying to wind down . . . and I like listening to you. You're very interesting, Carolyn, really. . . ."

"I'm not *that* interesting. Something else has pinned your interest, and I'll bet I know what it is." She took a long sip of her coffee, her eyes never leaving Judith's, as though she wasn't going to give Judith a chance to evade the truth.

"Carolyn, I . . . don't know what you mean . . . all I have is my business, and it's possible I've been preoccupied with it, but—"

"But then came Jason."

"Carolyn!"

"Oh, don't try to pretend. I happen to be a woman in love myself. I might be an old pregnant lady, but I know that look, Judith." Carolyn spoke with sincerity and softness that Judith couldn't buck.

"That's silly," she said in a flimsy effort to denounce what showed in her face. Her eyes lowered and she stared into the murky depths of her coffee.

"I knew it," Carolyn said. "Has there been something going on between you and my brother? I'm right, aren't I? You're more than just another subject, aren't you?"

Judith continued to stare into her coffee, and was dismayed to see rings form and vibrate outward as her tears fell into the mug. "I'm sorry . . . I feel so foolish. . . ."

Carolyn reached across the table and pressed her hand on Judith's arm. "Don't be ridiculous. You probably need a chance to let it out, don't you? Do you love my brother?"

Taken aback by Carolyn's bluntness, Judith couldn't hold in the tears that welled in her eyes, and her breath came in short sniffs. Helplessly she whispered, "Yes."

Carolyn leaned back. "That's all I need to know."

"What do you mean?"

"Oh, nothing, really. Jason's been involved with other women, but I haven't really met one that could convince me she loved him."

"Don't you believe me?"

"Judith, of course I believe you! That's my whole point. Jason's come home with plenty of women, and I was waiting for one who would say she loved him the way you just did: quietly. You know the old thing about protesting too much? Usually his 'affairs' are positively bubbling with declarations of their devotion."

Self-consciously Judith ventured, "How does Jason feel about these . . . affairs?"

Judith tensed as a sudden shawl came over the candidness in Carolyn's eyes. "I'd rather not pass judgment on that. Jason's very jealous of his privacy and he hides his feelings well when it comes to his lady friends. Sometimes his feelings are exactly opposite of the way he acts."

A shaft of anguish rammed through Judith, skewering heart, mind, body, and soul in a single thrust. Somehow she hid the torment from Carolyn; it was obvious Carolyn believed Jason wasn't returning Judith's desire and she wanted Judith to know she still had a chance at drawing his love. Little did Carolyn realize the truth, and the terrible impact of her words. Jason *was* returning Judith's desires already. Only now Judith knew that his declarations of love could be curtaining totally contrary feelings.

Carolyn was innocently going on. "I don't want to try comparing Jason's girls over all these years," she said, and Judith couldn't fault her for not wanting to be trapped. "But I'm not afraid to say I like you best. You're different. Maybe Jason will realize that too, in the end."

In the end.

The words pounded in Judith's ears. In a hopeless whisper she voiced, "It's already ended."

Carolyn blinked. "Did you say something, honey?"

It was fruitless to resist Carolyn's openness, and in moments, Judith's face was streaming with tears and she was whimpering the sad truth to Carolyn's sympathetic audience. "It's all over . . . before it hardly had a chance to begin. I love Jason . . . I tried not to, but it was something within me that refused to go away once it started. . . ." Her voice pittered away.

Carolyn pressed her arm again, reassuringly. "I don't understand, hon, why you're so upset. What could there be to come between you out there in the wilderness?"

"Victoria Phillips," she blurted desperately, "that's what."

Carolyn sat back in contemplation. "Victoria? That's funny. . . . I thought it was finished between them." She went on, unaware that she had just confirmed another horrible fear for Judith. Jason indeed had a past with Victoria, no doubt a romantic one. "I knew they had something going awhile ago, but . . . what makes you think Victoria's back in the picture?"

Judith sniffed and wrapped her hands around the warm mug. "My mind told me."

"You mean . . . you had a premonition about it?"

"As clear as crystal. I know it sounds ridiculous. I don't know what Jason has told you about my visions, but so far I haven't had one fail to be accurate or to come true. I

. . . I had a sharp vision of Jason with Victoria. I don't know any other way to interpret it except that Jason will end up leaving me to go back to her." Her sensibilities shattered and she covered her face with her hands, weeping uncontrollably and feeling completely foolish.

Carolyn dug through her purse for a travel packet of Puffs and pulled away one of Judith's hands to dab at her wet face like an attentive mother. "Oh, you poor kid," she murmured. "I could kick myself. I should've kept my big trap shut."

"It isn't your fault," Judith struggled between sobs. "You haven't told me anything I haven't already guessed or figured out. Or seen for myself in my mind." At once she looked up. "Promise me you won't say anything to Jason."

"Honey, I promise. I won't interfere any more than I already have. Jason's my brother and I love him, but if he can't see the value in a woman like you, he's the one who's losing."

"Oh, Carolyn, do you think he'll really go back to Victoria?"

Carolyn's face became stern and thoughtful. "I won't lie to you, Judith. Victoria is the only woman out of Jason's past who's still around. And I honestly don't know for sure if anything is brewing between the two of them. That doesn't mean there *is* something going on," she added hastily. "It just means I don't know. But if what you say is true . . ."

"It is," Judith moaned. "I saw it. My visions have been fading, less and less vivid each time, but the one that showed me Jason with Victoria was as lucid as a drive-in movie. I don't know how I'm going to make it through the summer knowing I'm going to lose him. It's going to be like waiting for a bomb to go off under me." The tears started to come again and she soaked them up with a tissue.

"Gee," Carolyn said, "I wish I could be more encouraging."

"It's all right, Carolyn. It's wonderful of you to care enough to listen. You're helping me more than you know. Please, Carolyn, you've got to promise again that you won't mention any of this to Jason! If he's going to make a life with Victoria, he deserves to do it without any guilt about me hanging over him."

With a heavy sigh, Carolyn leaned on her elbow and pursed her lips. "All this, and unselfish, too. Don't worry, sweetheart. I guess I've just put you through the third degree, but I won't butt in where I've been specifically asked not to do. Boy, sometimes I'd like to take that big lug of a brother of mine and kick him right in the libido. But listen." She leaned forward. "Any time you need a discerning ear to vent your feelings to, you just pick up that phone and call me. I'll even provide excuses for you to get away if you need to. We can spend the afternoon shopping or baking bread or something."

Judith dried her face and flipped a tissue in her glass of water. Tenderly she pressed the wetness against her hot cheeks and reddened eyes.

"You're a terrific friend, Carolyn. I'd forgotten how nice it could be to talk to a woman my own age. I can't thank you enough." Those last words almost choked her. As purging as it was to talk to Carolyn, it had also made Judith sure of her vision's accuracy.

The biggest challenge still remained: to keep Jason out of her bed—and to keep herself from wanting him there.

CHAPTER TWELVE

I haven't loved anyone since Lesley died.

I thought love was over for me . . . until you.

Life is full of surprises, Judith.

Vic and I have never had any trouble keeping each other occupied.

Jason's words thundered out of the past to crash and eddy like waves of a stormy sea in Judith's mind. She battled with her feelings, but nothing ever came out differently, including the ultimate conclusion. The final curtain always came down on Jason and Victoria walking arm in arm into the sunset.

The sweet honey of love was souring into a bitter cup, and she was unable to keep from resenting Jason's professions of love for her. No matter how sincere he seemed to be, the fact remained that he *had* loved many women since the death of his wife, that he had and apparently still loved Victoria, and that his intentions toward Judith consisted of satisfying his sexual appetite until the end of the summer when he would go back to Philadelphia, to Victoria, leaving still another male signature carved into Judith's maimed heart.

She was bailed out of sleeping with Jason for several days by a fluke of nature: she caught his cold. And she caught it good. It put her out of commission most of the next week and crowded the cabin with Peter and Peter's mother, Louisa. Peter and Jason took over the greenhouse, while Louisa strapped Judith to her bed and plied her with hot Jell-O-water and vegetable soup. Luckily for Judith, Louisa took no guff from menfolk and kept Jason and Peter from bothering her patient.

"Out! Out! Both of you!" she bellowed in a professional mother tone, shooing them out of the cabin. "Judith doesn't need you two clamoring around here. Go repair something or plant something, but stay out!"

"You're amazing, Louisa," Judith moaned from somewhere within the folds of her favorite quilt.

Louisa turned back to her, and a smile danced on her lovely Hispanic face. Louisa Viguera was a long way from the typical Spanish mama. She was slim even after five children, and still young, having married Sam at the tender age of seventeen and raised five terrific boys. The two eldest, twins, were twenty years old and off to college in West Virginia. At thirty-eight, Louisa kept a youthful lilt in her step, and with three kids still at home her attitudes were youthful, too. She always wore her jet-black pinstraight hair in the most modern cuts and always dived headlong into the newest innovations in running a household.

"I don't know how you do it," Judith said through a scratchy throat, "raising all those kids and Sam and taking care of me, too."

"Oh, poo," Louisa said, "You're hardly a nick in my daily routine. Besides, you're just about ready to get up and get active again. And you and my herd ain't seen nothin' from me yet. Wait till I get rid of Peter and Charlie, and Emilio's old enough to make his own lunch. I'm heading straight for the business world in high gear. I'm going to open up a boutique and gift shop in Bakerville right next to the expressway, and cater to all the world's travelers. The *rich* travelers with their Airstreams and motor homes. You just wait and see if I don't. Do you want your pillow fluffed up? How about a cup of golden-seal?"

Judith forced a sheepish smile. "As much as I preach the healing powers of goldenseal, I'd really curl up around a cup of black rum tea, if you don't mind the trouble."

"What trouble? I'll be right back. And I'll put on a record for you to listen to. What do you want to hear?"

"Let's see . . . take me to Florida. Put on Jimmy Buffet."

"No sooner said than did, kid," Louisa said, and lilted away, leaving Judith to think of how much Peter was like his mother. Judith nestled down into the pillow and closed her eyes, ready to lose herself in the folksy melodic plaints of Jimmy Buffet, and reflected on the fact that she felt ten times better today than she had in days. She thanked her lucky stars for the cold. It had kept Jason out of her bed. But now . . . ?

About the time when Jimmy Buffet was filling the air with lamentations about too many mobile homes in the Florida Keys, she heard a scratching at her window screen and looked in time to see the screen leap upward. Jason's handsome face invaded the room, and she was once again stricken by the impact of his strapping good looks.

"Hi, sickie," he said, leaning in farther. "I slipped past the guard."

"If she finds you in here, she'll hit you with a frying pan," Judith droned.

"I know. But I checked. She's making something for you to eat and she can't hear us talking over the music." He sat on the windowsill and one long leg followed the other into the room.

"Jason, I'd really rather rest than chat with you, if you don't mind."

"I do mind, my girl," he said forcefully. "It's time for you to get some fresh air. You've been cooped up in here for days now. You'll never get better if you don't get up and get moving. We city people have a few tricks up our

141

sleeves too, you know. We know how to force ourselves to get better." He was rummaging through her dresser drawer for a pair of jeans and a top. Once he found a thin flannel shirt with western-style embroidery, he pitched the clothing onto the bed. "Get up. Get dressed. I'm springing you." A smirk tugged at his lips, but there was no misinterpreting the keen glint of menace in his eyes that told her he was at his breaking point and no longer would be steered away from her.

Judith shrank under the defiance in his face and feebly reached for the clothing. He folded his arms and stood over her, one eyebrow cocked and his face only slightly mellowed by the remotest possibility of a grin shadowing his mouth. The more she looked at it, the less it looked like a grin.

In a stilted effort to control the inevitable, she said, "Would you mind letting me dress in private?"

For a moment he froze, as though the words had no meaning. Then he shifted his weight and blinked. "Did I hear you right?"

Guilt gnawed at her. "Yes."

"Are you telling me there's something about your lovely body that I have yet to encounter?"

"No . . ." she said quietly, "but I don't feel very lovely after spending so much time sick in bed. I'd rather not be watched while I'm dressing."

She dared to meet his regard, and it cooled her to see that the hint of grin was completely gone from his features. It was clear he suspected some underlying motive behind her request, and clear he didn't like it. He didn't like being told he wasn't welcome where he had decided he had a right to be. She saw the shadow of ownership in his hard eyes and knew he thought of her as his possession, a conquest he had taken and still held.

Icily he made his decision. "All right. But hurry it up." He started toward the window.

142

Resentment bubbled within Judith. She still felt cranky from the cold's lingering, and her lips pressed together in a surge of anger. "On second thought, I think I'll stay right where I am, like I wanted to in the first place."

She winced when his eyes pierced her again. A tense moment crawled by.

"Get dressed, Judith. I'm tired of seeing you curled up like an invalid. You've had enough bed rest and you need to get your blood flowing. I'll be back in five minutes, and I expect to see you out of that bed and ready to take a walk." His tone was callous, his eyes still iron hard, without pity. She was sure of it now—he sensed her wish to remain apart from him, physically and emotionally.

He did come back in five minutes, almost to the second, and stood at the window without saying a word—a most ominous silence. Judith obediently allowed him to assist her over the sill. His hands were curiously lacking in gentility as he grasped her ribcage and lifted her down to the grass.

"Come on," he ordered, clutching her arm.

They walked in silence until they passed the meadow creek, when Jason said, "You're not sneezing much, Judith." His meaning was undisguised.

"That doesn't mean I feel all that well," she clipped back at him as though she had been expecting his comment.

He slipped an arm around her waist and casually tried to draw her against him, but unwilling to relax, she bumped his firm side and levered away from him. She kept walking, fighting the compulsion to meet his eyes as they bored into her flesh.

"What's the matter with you, anyway?" he asked bluntly.

"Why should anything be the matter?"

"For one, you've been treating me like a complete

stranger since we went to Bakerville. Did you discover something about me there that you didn't like?"

"No—" she said, too hastily. "Why would you think that? I mean . . . I don't know where you would get that idea. . . ."

"I get that idea from the fact that you've been avoiding me as though I'm surrounded by a swarm of locusts. Not very flattering, Judith."

"I've . . . I've been sick, you know. Colds hit me hard and I usually don't prefer to see anyone."

Jason stopped walking and pulled her around to squarely face him.

"That's the problem, isn't it?"

"I don't know what you mean. . . ."

"What you just said, my dear girl." His eyes grew cold and dangerous, shaded from the sunlight by a swatch of darkly glistening hair. "I thought I rated as more than just 'anyone.' It disturbs me to hear myself lumped into that category. I'd like to know the reason behind it. And I'd also like to know if I'm going to be welcome in your bedroom tonight, now that you're feeling better."

She quivered under his glare, unwillingly facing the demand there. Was there no limit to his bluntness? Why did she feel as though she were denying him something that belonged to him?

It seemed he was reading her thoughts, as though her mind was pared open by his will alone, open to his study like a common magazine. As though he knew she had no answer ready, he pressed on relentlessly.

"I told you I'll never beg for love, never lower myself to prove to anyone what my feelings are." He gripped her arms tighter and stood over her, bare inches away, with the sun creating a magical aureole around his body that blinded her to everything but his raw power. "I want to know if you want me, and I want to know now."

His breath was hot on her face, and desperately Judith

tried to back away from his steel grip. "Please . . . you've got to give me time. . . ."

"Is that a no?"

"Jason—"

"Don't play with me, Judith. I'm not a toy to be tossed aside. I've noticed a distinct change in your attitude toward me, sensed it if nothing more, and there's got to be a reason." He bombarded her with his words, merciless to the helpless expression on her face. "Has something changed your mind about my ability to satisfy you? Is that what you're telling me?"

Barely managing to break his grip, Judith moved a few steps away, trying to put a buffer zone between them. She was surprised that he had let her go, and fought to assimilate her roiling senses. Even in the discomfort of the moment, his very presence charged her with thrills she could hardly hide, a current of primitive desire that rooted from the deepest of impulses, that no woman wanted to admit to.

"I'm telling you that I would like to retain some control over my life. I don't see why you should be so upset." Her tone was as hollow as a Ping-Pong ball, and she knew it, but he had trapped her with his perceptiveness.

His eyes narrowed to catlike ferocity.

"You *don't*?" he snapped baldly. "You don't see how your words cut into me?" He straightened his back and his voice grew dry. "You're more callous than I would have given you credit for, Judith. How you can be proud of it is beyond me."

Her mind cried out to him as he wheeled around and stalked away with a steady pace that was evidence of his refusal to be shamed, but this time the echo went no farther than the confines of her own skull, where it bounced around in futility. By the time Jason had vanished around the crest of a hill, a throbbing ache had kindled and fired in her head that had nothing to do with her cold. She sank down on a tree stump, clasped her hands between her knees, and turned her face to the comfortless warmth of the sun. She could only hope it would at least dry the tears.

Louisa was positively livid when Judith finally wandered back to the cabin, constantly on the lookout for Jason. But he was nowhere to be seen. At first Judith was relieved, but then a pang of sadness lanced her and she knew that she had turned away her last chance for love, all because it would only be a matter of time before he would be taken from her. Would she ever again have the courage to allow a man's touch on her body, a man's passionate domination of her senses, a man's romantic image filling her mind? Could she ever bring herself to chance being hurt all over again?

Louisa was standing at the door when she arrived.

"You little delinquent," she scolded. "I ought to turn you over my knee and spank you. Where did you go?"

"Jason made me take a walk with him. I'm sorry, Lou."

"Playing hooky, huh? Well, I guess you do look a little rosier. Maybe the sun and fresh air did you some good. Come on in and I'll give you your lunch before I go. Where's your partner in crime?"

"Isn't he here?" Judith asked, trying to keep the giveaway tremor from her voice.

"If he is, I haven't seen him. He probably didn't want to face the music for spiriting you away." Louisa flashed a smile from within her flawless deep-gold Spanish complexion, and shooed Judith inside. She set two bowls on the table, filled them with hot brown rice and spooned vegetable curry over it. The spicy aroma filled the kitchen with a Middle Eastern flavor and momentarily floated Judith away from her plaguing thoughts.

Louisa paused a moment and scanned Judith's face.

"You should wash your face with cool water and rinse your eyes, kid. They're as red as valentines."

Sputtering, Judith forced herself to respond. "Oh . . . I will. Thanks." She knew the true reason her eyes were red, and the sadness tumbled back into place.

"What's the matter?" Louisa asked. "Something wrong?"

Quickly, Judith said, "No, nothing . . . I don't feel quite up to par yet, that's all."

"I know. You'll feel draggy for a while yet, but at least it's not the middle of winter and you can get out into the fresh outdoors. Well, I've got to go. I have to drive Emilio to his piano lesson. He hates to be late, so I'd better exit. For an eight-year-old, he sure takes things seriously."

Judith sighed. "With that attitude, he'll be a virtuoso musician someday. Thanks for hovering over me for the past few days, Louisa. It's great to have special friends around to worry about me."

Louisa laughed and headed for the door. "Wait till Sam and all the boys come down with the flu. Guess who I'll pin for help!"

When Louisa had gone, Judith sat alone with a cup of tea steaming her face for what seemed to be a long time. The sun actually changed its position in the time she was sitting there and streamed in the cabin windows to create a golden warmth that felt especially good right now. She let her mind wander into a void. All thoughts were dominated by Jason now, so she was glad to let her mind relax and empty itself of the tedious quandary. She was suddenly in doubt of her decision to alienate Jason's affections for the remainder of his stay, but what else could she do? She couldn't allow herself to be a pawn in his game, later to be cast aside, but to deny the fierce desire that rose within her and the wild song her body sang when he was near—who was the real loser? Jason and Victoria would have each other, and Judith . . .

She shook her head. There seemed to be no peace from it, no sanctuary into which thoughts of Jason did not follow. Would it be like this forever? Would the pain never go away? Or would it fade for a time, only to surge up again whenever some small reminder confronted her? Even more so than women who spend their lives with no love at all, she was love's toy, beaten and battle weary, cast aside over and over to rot in some dark corner until the painful cycle began again. No, it was not better to have loved and lost. It was worse, much worse. At least people who were spared love's barbs could learn to embellish the art of singleness, to live full lives by learning to wake up not alone, but with themselves. Judith's cherished aloneness had withered to loneliness. Such a terrible difference.

She jumped involuntarily when the screen door flew open and Peter sauntered in.

"Hi."

"Hi, Peter."

"How you feeling?"

Judith shrugged. "So-so. Better, I suppose."

"Hit that medium-yuck stage, huh?" He slid into a chair and folded his scrawny arms. Fledgling muscles bundled like ripening fruit under the skin of his upper arms, and Judith saw again the raw makings of a strong tall man building there. The thought blundered in that she would probably never have the chance to raise a son of her own. Never . . .

"Where's Jace, anyway?" Peter asked innocently.

"I don't know," she answered in an empty tone. "Haven't you seen him?"

"Huh-uh. Not since he said he was gonna spring you from my mom. Is she still here?"

"No, she had to go—"

"Oh, yeah, I forgot. Emilio's piano lesson is today. Can I eat dinner with you and Jace?"

"Oh, Peter, I dearly wish you would!"

He blinked.

"How come you said it that way?"

She paused to look for an answer, then honesty decided to surface. Peter was just about the oldest friend she had in the world. Treating him like a child wouldn't be fair.

"I don't feel like being alone with Jason right now, Pete. I could use somebody to run interference for me."

"I don't get it?" His young face screwed up in confusion. "I thought you and Jace were . . . you know."

She gazed into her cooling tea. "It's . . . not working out between Jason and me. Sometimes things don't go the way you hope they will."

A protective duskiness crossed Peter's face that was probably the most adult expression Judith had seen him wear to date. He leaned forward on folded arms, and stared seriously at the single beaded tear that swelled in her left eye and refused to fall. It sat there on her eyelashes, catching sunlight and telling Peter how affected Judith was by this turn of circumstance.

"You like him a whole lot, though. Don't you?" he asked, trying to piece it all together. "I mean, you sorta love him, don't you? I thought you did. The way you guys were acting. Boy, I don't like this." He got up and paced the floor.

Rousing herself, Judith said, "Peter, don't let it get to you," she said in a lighter tone. "I've been through this before. I'll survive." She didn't tell him about the scars that became harder and harder to bear each time around.

"I don't get it," Peter went on. "And I don't like it. It must be his fault. I bet you didn't do anything. You're too nice. Man, if I were four years older . . ."

Judith allowed herself a small laugh, hoping he would notice it. "What could you do? Challenge him to a duel? American history at twenty paces?"

"I'd cream him." He jammed an oversized adolescent

149

fist into his other palm. "Nobody hurts your feelings when I'm around."

Judith shook her head and smiled. "Peter . . . you're too loyal for your own good, aren't you?" She went to him and draped her arm over his bony shoulders. "You've got to understand. Just because two people can share love, it doesn't mean they can share a life together. I wish things could be different too, but . . . we don't always get what we want."

Peter stood up tall and leered wisely at her. "But you wanted to be with Jace. I could tell. It doesn't seem very fair to me."

She sighed. "No . . . but fairness isn't anything that gets doled out in equal parcels." She wiped the tear out of her eye with a bent knuckle and knew she was failing to hide her misery from him.

Peter was stewing about this discovery; Judith could see it simmering behind his resolute expression, ready to boil at the slightest rising of the flame. "Don't fret too long, Peter. I'll get over it . . . I promise." She hoped he couldn't see the lingering pain behind the falseness of her words.

"Yeah . . . but you shouldn't have to. What a rat he is. I thought he was a neat person and I even told him I wanted to be like him, but I think I'm going to have a change of heart."

Mentally and physically drained, Judith nestled into the overstuffed chair. "That's your decision, Pete. But remember . . . relationships aren't guaranteed to go smoothly. Maybe it's not all Jason's fault. Maybe I shouldn't have let the whole thing get started." She looked back on Jason's first touch, his first kiss, the first rapturous blaze of sensation that jolted her quiet world and sent her reeling into orbit. She saw herself painted against the mosaic of Jason's multifaceted temperament, his sultry tenderness and raging passion.

"Then whose fault is it?"

"Peter," she admonished sternly. "I'm trying to impress you with my sage wisdom. You're not cooperating."

"Okay. I'll shut up. But it's gonna be a 'specially nasty silence. If he doesn't treat you right, I'm big enough to sock him right in the kneecap."

He succeeded in making her laugh again, this time sincerely. His anger subsided as he realized he had been upsetting her, and he sat on the hammock and swung back and forth.

"Hey," Judith began quietly. "I need help from you."

"Yeah? Like what?"

"Like I need you to be cheerful tonight. Pretend you don't know anything about this. Help me keep some kind of conversation going so it's not like a tomb in here. Will you do me that favor?"

Peter grinned self-consciously. "Tough act. But I'll try."

"Then it's a deal?" She offered her hand.

He took it and said, "Yeah. It's a deal. But wait till you get my bill."

CHAPTER THIRTEEN

Good old Peter.

He did a terrific job of acting that evening, though traces of disgruntlement did break the surface from time to time. Jason was stoic, Judith was uncomfortable, and dinner was short. Jason retired early to the loft on some feeble excuse of reading or doing some paperwork, and Judith tried to keep her sigh of relief from echoing too loudly. She had to hide her amusement at Peter's new-found prowess when he announced he was spending the night in the hammock and strutted the cabin floor like a peacock guarding his nest. She dared not shatter his pride by telling him he needn't stay, so he spent the night hunting the two cats around the furniture and between the houseplants while Cashel headed them off at the passes.

The next morning, Peter hovered attentively through breakfast, not allowing Jason to be alone with Judith for more than a couple of minutes at a time. Luckily, it was a weekend, and he didn't have to rush off to school. Eventually Jason went outside, carrying an armful of books and trade journals, apparently preferring the open spaces and sunlight to the coolness of atmosphere in the cabin. Only then did Peter head for the greenhouse to prepare last year's seeds for outdoor planting.

Judith spent her morning wrapped in a cloak of despair, unable to concentrate fully on the task of melting, scenting, and molding candlewax that she had set as the day's work.

As noon rolled around and the sun came once again to her windows, her thoughts wandered toward whether she should make lunch or wait until Jason decided to come in. How could she go on like this? The tension was killing, and it had only been one day. How could she live through the weeks to come, trying to live this mockery?

Her thoughts were broken by a knock at the cabin door. Common sense told her it wasn't Peter or Jason; they wouldn't knock. Or was this Jason's way of showing his bitterness?

As she went to the door and saw a strange man in a blue sports jacket, she felt bad about her low estimation of Jason.

"Yes? Can I help you?" she asked, hiding the feeling of sheepishness.

"Are you Judith Longfellow?"

"Yes."

"My name's Joe Holloway. I'm with Sanborn Financial Services."

Her stomach knotted out of habit. "Oh. . . ."

"You owe us some money, Judy." He said it with much too much personal inflection, and took two steps forward.

"I know that," she said.

"Four back payments, to be exact," Holloway went on as though she had said nothing. "It wasn't easy to get all the way back here, and I'd like to take the money with me when I go. How do you feel about that?" The sunlight did its best to improve dusty pale hair and a pock-marked face, but he squinted away from it.

Stepping out onto the chipped cement porch, Judith began, "Well . . . I feel fine about it, except that I don't . . . exactly have the money to give you yet. Not that much. But I'm going to have it—all of it—in just a few weeks."

"Oh, really? How's that?"

153

She hesitated, and a warm sweat broke out on the back of her neck. Oh, how she hated being in debt! "You see, I'm getting a grant in a matter of a few weeks. A research grant."

"You can't pay us with money meant for research. Don't play me for an idiot. A pretty lady like you should know better than that."

"I didn't mean that," she said hastily. "I mean . . . I'm the research. Someone is studying me and I'm getting paid for it."

"Uh-huh."

"I'm telling you the truth!"

"Okay. Where's this money coming from?"

"The McNair Institute for Parapsychical Study in Philadelphia."

Joe Holloway's lips pursed in total disbelief. Judith saw she was getting nowhere fast and desperately added, "I'm psychic."

"Oh, come on, lady," Holloway blurted, cocking his hip. "You expect me to swallow that malarkey? You're asking me to wait weeks for my company's money because somebody is paying you to read minds or something?" He took another step forward, ominously, as though meaning to threaten her.

"I do expect you to believe it," she said quickly, "because it's true. You'll be paid in full as soon as I get my stipend. Now please go away."

The screen door slapped closed behind her as she stalked back inside, fuming at the world's general lack of compassion and trust. Was there no escape from the callousness of the outside world?

There seemed not to be.

As she reached the stove where a pot of paraffin was slowly bubbling, she whirled to the sound of the screen door bumping closed again. Joe Holloway was standing

154

inside the cabin, watching her reaction with a leering kind of amusement.

"What are you doing?" Judith demanded. "I didn't invite you in!"

"I know you didn't," Holloway said, moving slowly to the edge of the counter. "But I'm not supposed to leave here without some . . . payment."

An alarm went off in Judith's head and made her feel suddenly defenseless. She stiffened. "I told you. I don't have any money to give you right now."

He leaned with far too much familiarity on the counter and the leering cast in his eyes took on a frightening sharpness. "Hey," he said, with a snarly kind of pseudo-friendliness. "Why don't we be friends, eh? You scratch my back, I'll scratch yours. I mean, hey, you're a good-looking woman, Judy. Maybe we can arrange some . . . let's call it a facsimile for payment."

Trembling with fear and fury, Judith hissed, "I don't know what you're talking about! I want you to leave. I'll mail you the money I owe your company as soon as I get it. Now get out!"

"Oh, c'mon, baby." He approached her like a snake and only then did she realize he was almost as big as Jason. There was no chance of her contending with him physically, and certainly not in the way he expected.

Judith wanted to look out the window to see if anyone was near enough to answer a cry for help, but it was impossible to tear her eyes away from Holloway's devious face. She backed away, around the kitchen table. "I want you out of here," she said, trying to sound powerful. "If you don't get out now, I won't pay your company anything at all, and I'll have a reason not to!"

"I've heard that line before, baby. You gals never mean what you say." He reached for her hand, but she dodged away like a bird from a cat's pounce and lunged toward the door.

155

But he was faster.

He sidestepped back around the table and caught her in the middle of the room, locking her in a solid grip. "There now. Isn't this better?"

"Let go of me!"

The acrid scent of too-strong cologne infused her nostrils and she twisted desperately in his grip, to no avail.

She tried to kick Holloway, but he pushed her off balance and caused her to stumble, still holding her arms, and forced her back against the counter. The Formica cut into her lower back as she squirmed uselessly. He said, "Don't fight too long, baby. I might decide to fight back."

"Stop it! Let me go!" Her voice tore from her throat as the sickening sensation of his face nuzzling into her neck lanced her with revulsion. "Let me *go!*"

Her shriek bounced around the kitchen and masked the sound of the screen door creaking open. In seconds Holloway's weight was torn off her and she staggered into a corner. She caught a swift glimpse of Jason's balled fists flashing and her assailant flew raggedly across the table and crashed into a chair, landing in a heap on the kitchen floor.

Jason bent over briefly and came up with Holloway's lapels in his fists and the collector hanging from them like a fish on a hook.

"I hope I was mistaken about what I thought I saw going on here," Jason growled into Holloway's astonished face.

"Hey . . . man . . . I didn't know! She . . . she was leading me on! I didn't know she was cheating on somebody! Honest, pal!"

Judith's lips fell open in disbelief, but she was unable to force a sound out of her clenched throat as Holloway babbled on.

"I came to get my company's money, but she said she

had a better way to pay me. Typical, huh? Just like a woman—"

Jason tossed him toward the door, his massive bulk standing dangerously tall, dwarfing even Holloway's big frame as the collector cringed away.

"Your company will get its money and you will consider yourself lucky to still have a job."

A last-ditch snicker blinked on Holloway's face. "You couldn't get me fired. You can't prove anything."

"Maybe not. But you wouldn't be much use to your company with your legs in your ears. I'll walk you to your car, friend."

"Yeah, yeah, I'm going. Don't push."

"Move."

Jason clamped his arm and steered Holloway out the door, then watched diligently as the invader got in his car, rather contritely, and drove away. When Jason came back in the cabin, his face was limned with smokey anger. He glared at Judith with a tinge of hatefulness lacing his eyes.

"Did he hurt you?"

She had to swallow before she could breathe. A piercing need to rush into the comfort of his strong arms washed through her, but his heartless expression and the sheer anathema in his darkened eyes was like a steel wall springing up between them.

"No," she murmured, her voice quivering a weak treble.

He grunted. "Good thing I came in when I did. Why did you let him at all?"

She felt her voice rising. "You can't mean you believe what he said!"

"I don't know what to believe anymore, Judith," he said. Each word was clipped and distinct, hammering in the syllables, cutting him totally adrift from any concern for her feelings. "Maybe I don't understand women as well as I thought I did. I seem to keep running up against surprises."

Suddenly, pure anger rose up in her, a violent reaction to his damned cocky snobbery. How dared he be angry at *her*?

"If you thought I led him on, why did you interfere at all?" she heard herself demand. "I certainly don't need you to be fighting my battles for me, Jason."

A maelstrom of conflicting shadows crossed his face, bringing to it a feral recklessness that threatened to tear her heart from her body and pummel it to a hopeless writhing mass on the floor. When it came, his voice was a low thunder rumbling from his throat, a terrible storm moving in to dash her to splinters.

"You certainly know how to accept a favor gracefully, don't you?"

He lumbered toward her methodically, his fist balled in pent-up rage. "You refuse to let things go smoothly, don't you? You're determined that the ten thousand dollars come right out of my hide, aren't you, Judith? I should have known better than to think you were different. You're no different at all."

He turned and tensions tugged at the muscles of his back as he drifted across the floor to stand in the bathing sunlight from a plant-laden window.

The ensuing silence was crushing.

In trembling self-defense, Judith pursued him. "You've got your nerve passing any kind of judgment on me, Jason. I thought you were capable of respecting me on a mutual level. I gave you credit for being more than an average chauvinist male, but you've proven me wrong. If it weren't for the money, I—"

"You what?" He whirled on her. "You'd throw me out? Is the money all that's kept you interested in me?" He approached, and his tall form cast a shadow on her. "You

158

mercenary little bitch——that's all I am to you! Ten thousand bucks."

"Yes!" she lied furiously, immediately wishing she could bite back the words. But she was committed to her own rage now, and attacked him with her own resentment of herself for letting him so dominate her life. "If it weren't for the money, I would have thrown you out on your ear the first moment I saw you! Is that what you want to hear? Go ahead and believe anything you like. Apparently you will anyway, no matter what I say."

"As a matter of fact, I detect far too much sincerity behind your sarcasm," he said with a bitter sneer.

"Just because you've had my body doesn't mean you've miraculously changed me into a promiscuous harlot who sells herself to the highest bidder! Not even for ten thousand dollars!" She felt the skin on her neck heating beneath the heavy fall of hair. Her arms were stiff, her legs locked, fighting the voice within her that constantly repeated *you love him . . . don't do this*. All the tension and self-deprecation was boiling to the top now, and she was helpless to stop it from spilling into the fire and scalding them both, leaving only the red-hot ash of love gone wrong. "I hate you, Jason, and I hate myself for ever loving you or ever believing you could really love me! You're like every other man under the skin——a user of women!"

His eyes blazed as though they had caught her fire and in a thought he jerked her into his arms and glared down into the pools of her eyes. They heard the sibilant rising of steam as the flame in his eyes struck the ice in hers. He yanked her against his rough body and growled, "You're handicapped, my girl. You're surrounded by a thorny wall of memories that you haven't even tried to climb. You figure you're safe in there, but you're very wrong. That wall will protect you to death, Judith. It'll smother every genuine feeling you might have had. You'll live with your-

159

self until you can't stand to look in the mirror. And then you'll look back and remember that you could've had this."

He crushed her in a pinioning embrace and captured her mouth in a punitive, brutal kiss. His lips bruised her as he drew out the punishment, one hand breaking free to invade the looseness of the khaki spring shirt she wore, to take possession of a tautening breast.

Hatred merged with undeniable desire as Judith weakened under the sensuous demand he elicited from her body. She could barely breathe under the relentless exploration of his mouth on hers, and her head reeled as he tipped her backward enough to put her balance in his complete control.

His hand was a traveler roaming the terrain of her breasts, tantalizing the tender skin, echoing the movements of his tongue as it probed and plunged deeply into the cavern of her response.

Mesmerized, she let it go on, hardly aware of time passing or anything existing outside the realm of Jason's incendiary teasing of her stiff nipples, hardly able to recall why she despised herself so at this moment. An indecent shock sliced through her body as cleanly as if it carried voltage.

She barely sensed the slow metamorphosis in Jason. His cruel, demanding motions became urgent caresses, his crushing kiss mellowing to tender immediacy. "Judith—" His hot breath gusted in a whisper, a beckoning request to forget the anger and allow the loving to begin again.

But she couldn't allow it to begin again. She knew she would never be able to turn back, never be able to say no if she didn't say no now. Could she live with herself either way—?

"No—!" she choked, leaning as far away from him as his grasp would allow. "No, Jason—I can't let you—"

Her voice stuck in her throat when his body flushed ice cold against her.

"Can't let me what? Use you? We're back to that?" His voice was still thick with the huskiness of arousal, but his eyes had crusted as hard as dry bone.

In fitful defense she said, "I don't owe you any explanations." Then, unplanned—"I want you out of my house—today! Now!"

She levered away from him and smoothed her wrinkled shirt down over territory he had too nearly conquered again. Her words surprised even her, and the moments hung in raw suspension as they stared at each other, waiting for Fate's next turn.

His tone snaked along the floor. "You mean that?"

She couldn't bring herself to answer.

Jason's shoulders slumped momentarily, then squared. "Yes, I can see you do." He backed away a single telling step. "I'll be gone in fifteen minutes, Judith. I assume there's nothing more to be said."

A shadow that might have been sorrow swathed his features as he spun and vanished into the corridor. The loft ladder creaked under his weight, and the sound of his footsteps on the carpeted floor up there rumbled down as he gathered his belongings.

Judith felt her face redden and her eyes swell, her chest tighten and her throat knot. Before the tears burst from her eyes, she broke out of the cabin and ran aimlessly into the meadow toward the river. She caught a glimpse of Peter watching her as she passed the greenhouse, but in her misery and humiliation there was no room to explain to him what had happened. She could only hope her caring young friend had enough finesse to sense that she needed to be alone much more than she needed company.

161

CHAPTER FOURTEEN

It seemed impossible.

How could he be gone?

How could a life that once had been so vibrant and full now be so desolate? How could the warmth of the sun be so bleak, so heavy with memories?

Jason had been right; Judith was confined behind a wall of memories, locked in the chains of her own past. And now she had one more tragic memory to add to her private prison.

When she had cried herself to a wrinkled pulp and her jeans were soaked to the knees from where she had sat on the bank and let her feet dangle in the river's shallow water, she let her face accept the sun's heat that dried the tears in their tracks. The streaks remained on her cheeks as she wandered absently along the riverbank and then back toward home.

It was as though she were afraid to go back. Something within her cringed away, telling her that if she didn't go home maybe none of this would ever have happened and her business, her life, would be safe from the nightmare. She stood beneath a waving birch sapling, surveying with misty eyes her distant cabin, the steamy greenhouse, the tiny form of Peter working in the area that would be planted for an outside herb garden. Would *have* been— now, what would be the point of carrying out the pretense of keeping The Calico Patch in operation? She couldn't possibly put a big enough dent in her debts before her creditors foreclosed on her loans. Not now . . . not without the money Jason's institute would have paid her. Even if they decided to pay her an appropriate amount for the time he had stayed, it wouldn't be enough.

There was precious little hope of any alternatives, and in her depressed state Judith couldn't even imagine any chance of saving her life's work. She hardly wanted to bother; what was the point? There would be no sweet Jason to share it with, no strong protective arms to fall asleep in, no broad shoulders to caress in the night, no male legs to tangle in her own, no one to wake up to each bright morning.

Life for Judith would have to start all over again. Could she build her business all over again from nothing? At least the first time she had had the money her mother had saved for Judith's college education. She had invested that money in her patch of fertile land and begun payments on the cabin and greenhouse. Would she lose her land now too? Probably—the property and buildings were the most valuable single commodities she owned. A collection agency wouldn't be interested in the business itself.

She felt strangely numb, detached from it all. There seemed to be no difference between life with her business or life without it. All life was without Jason, and therefore barren.

Dull to sensation itself, she almost didn't notice Peter come to her side when she finally wandered near the cabin.

"Hi," he said uneasily.

Forcing herself to respond, Judith managed, "Hi."

"Jace is gone," Peter said, squinting into the sun.

"I know."

"I told him off."

A glimmer of consciousness broke through the torpor. "You told him off? What do you mean?"

He looked at the ground and shrugged, deciding

163

whether to be proud or ashamed of himself. "You know what I mean. I told him you didn't need him or his money." Then he looked up abruptly. "And you don't!" he said emphatically. "You've got me, and my mom and dad. And I've got some money saved up. I'll get another job, part-time, someplace else. I can work here on weeknights and the other job on weekends. And I'll give you all the money so you won't have to give up the business. We can do it, Judith, I know we can!"

His enthusiasm touched a place deep inside her, awakening the tiny frozen core of her heart, and she smiled at him. Though her dreams were lying splintered on the ground, she couldn't bring herself to destroy his, or to rob him of this ultimate generosity. "Maybe we can, Pete," she said, knowing she was lying.

"I knew you wouldn't give up!" Peter bubbled. "I'll start looking for another job tomorrow. We'll get out of this somehow. We'll show him! He's not gonna walk all over us without a fight, is he?"

"No . . . no, of course not. I appreciate your loyalty, Peter, I truly do. You're a fine man."

He blushed, but walked a bit straighter.

Judith forced the grin to stay on her face, but doubted she was hiding it from him. Could he detect the crushing weight of soured love slumping her shoulders? She assumed he could; in fact, she was sure of it. She wasn't putting much over on Peter. He was too astute to miss it.

For several days Judith continued to fill her standing orders and allowed Peter to begin planting the outside garden, more for Peter's sake than anything else. Meanwhile, she began the arduous, disheartening task of adding up her net worth and projecting her profit over the weeks to come, to see whether or not she could save some parcel of her business, or be driven into bankruptcy.

One morning, while Peter was at school, Judith stood outside the cabin, relishing the warm dampness of an overcast day. The air was muggy—a welcome feeling after the coolness of spring. The sun glowed dimly behind a textured wall of cloud, and in the distance a percussion of thunder promised rain—lots of rain. A good soaking would nourish the Allegheny Mountains and coax broad green leaves from the buds.

She let a heavy breeze lift the hair from her neck and caress her tense shoulders with its warm invisible arms. It felt good, terribly good. The simplicity of nature was doing its best to assure her that any wound could heal in time. Even the rattling bare branches of winter would be fertile again, it told her. Somehow, she would have to survive.

She was leaning back against the shed, her face raised, her eyes closed, and her arms folded, when the sound of a car with a bad muffler registered on her ears and she noticed a station wagon lumbering down the road toward her. She ignored it, then she recognized Carolyn's late model station wagon.

A hand came out of the driver's window and waved at her as the car pulled up. Carolyn had Dori in her arms when she got out. "Hi, Judith!"

"Hi—what a nice surprise!" Judith fought to disguise the fact that she was quaking within. Had Jason sent Carolyn? If so, why?

Cashel bounded up to greet Dori, who reached out and giggled, "Apple!"

"Apple?" Carolyn asked.

"That's as close as she could get to his name," Judith explained. "It's Cashel."

"Hey, dinky, that's pretty close!" Carolyn put the toddler on the ground and let her wander around with the delighted setter. "We were shopping for a birthday dress, and I got the bug to visit you. Hope you don't mind a surprise."

"Oh, no! I'm glad to see you, Carolyn. It gets pretty

165

quiet around here sometimes." Funny—she never minded the quiet before.

"I'll say," Carolyn laughed. "I had to stop up the road twice to ask where you live. You're really secluded out here. It sure is beautiful countryside though. I'll bet I have time for a cup of coffee before we have to get back."

"Oh, Carolyn, I'd love it if you would. Come on in."

Over steaming cappuccino and doughnuts, the two women shared a comfortable chat, and Judith was relieved that the tears stayed inside instead of breaking out for no reason as they so often did these days.

"Is it my imagination, or are you thinner than before?" Carolyn asked candidly.

"Maybe a pound or two . . ."

"You haven't been eating."

"Sure . . . I eat."

Carolyn hit her with that look that Judith couldn't lie to. "Eating how much?"

A sheepish grin touched Judith's lips. "Not much, I admit. But a short fast is very healthy."

Carolyn ignored her excuse. "Food's not very appetizing right now, huh?"

"Not very. How do you get these things out of me that I wasn't going to tell anyone?"

With a wink, Carolyn said, "Don't ever believe there's no such thing as feminine intuition."

"With you around? Let me pour you some more cappuccino before you get me crying again."

"Crying's good for you," Carolyn added with a nod. "Gee, is that thunder I hear?"

"It's been coming this way all morning. We're in for a typical mountain spring downpour."

"Hm. I'd better have one more cup and get going. I don't want to get stranded if the river comes up over the road anywhere. Where is that kid of mine anyway?" She looked out the window. "She could be in Toledo by now, the way she wanders."

"I see her," Judith said, "out in my garden with Cashel."

"Oh, Judith—I'll get her!"

"No, no, let her play. She can't hurt anything. The seeds are planted good and deep. She seems to be enjoying herself. She's covering Cashel's face with topsoil."

"What a tolerant dog!"

"Are you kidding? He thinks he died and went to heaven."

Carolyn sipped her cappuccino and gazed thoughtfully at a doughnut. "Seems like everyone in this house is a little more tolerant than necessary." She looked now directly at Judith. "And, no, Jason doesn't know I'm here."

Judith felt the heat rise in her face.

"I know," Carolyn said, "you've been trying to ask without really asking. How've you been holding up, hon?"

"Well enough," Judith sighed. "I know I can't fool you, so I won't say I've forgotten Jason or what he means to me."

"Still love him, then?"

"I think I always will."

Carolyn crossed her legs and thought a moment. "Maybe you were mistaken about your vision, Judith. Don't you think that's possible?"

Judith shrugged and sat down after pouring more cappuccino. "It's possible. But I'd be fooling myself to think so. I can't take the chance. It's painful enough to lose him now. What would it be like if I let it go on, only to lose him later? It would be that much more horrible for me."

"But then, at least you'd have your stipend," Carolyn suggested, not very convincingly, then changed her mind. "I suppose money doesn't really compensate if you love someone that deeply."

A lump clogged Judith's throat. "It's not only that,

167

Carolyn. I would be taking the money under false pretenses."

"Why would you say that?"

"To be honest . . . I'm sure now that the injury that made me psychic has healed. Remember I told you the images were getting fewer and fewer?"

"I remember."

Judith had more difficulty voicing her realization than she expected. "They're completely gone now. There wouldn't be anything for Jason to study even if he did come back."

"Are you that sure of it?"

Slowly Judith nodded. "Unless Jason really loved me, there wouldn't be anything for him here anymore." Tears flooded her eyes.

Carolyn waited through a thoughtful pause. "Jason hasn't been saying much, so I can't tell you what he's thinking. Mostly he plays with Dori and helps Brian get around. He and Brian have been shooting pool at the local hangout, but other than that he's a blank screen. I wish I could be more encouraging."

Judith smiled listlessly, but gratefully. "Carolyn . . . I appreciate your being honest with me. It wouldn't do any good to delude myself. Jason is going to end up with someone else, no matter how I wish it could be different."

Carolyn peered suspiciously at the darkening sky and said, "Well, I've got to scoot. It looks like it's going to burst a seam up there. Those mountain roads around Bakerville are treacherous enough without trying to navigate them in the rain."

"Thanks for coming, Carolyn," Judith said sincerely. "It's wonderful to feel like somebody cares as much as you do. It makes me feel better about myself."

"I'm glad you think so," Carolyn said as she led the way outside. "I wasn't sure if you wanted me around, dragging back all the memories. Come on, Dori! Time to go home, see Daddy."

"It wouldn't do me any good to pretend it never happened," Judith admitted, "especially if it means pretending I didn't have friends like you."

Carolyn smiled, retrieved her tiny daughter, and strapped the child into her safety seat. "Remember . . . anytime you need to talk to somebody, I'm your gal. Don't hesitate. Even if we can't be sisters-in-law, nobody can keep us from being buddies."

Judith reached out impulsively and met Carolyn in a warm hug.

" 'Bye, hon, and take care," Carolyn murmured.

"Thanks again, Carolyn. You're the best."

"Yeah, I know!"

Clinging to any piece of Jason that was left in her life, Judith felt slightly more human as she watched the station wagon waddle down the road and out of sight. How terrific Carolyn was, driving all the way out here from Baker-ville just to check on her. She'd been rather vague about Jason; obviously he wasn't interested in showcasing his feelings one way or the other. Judith was reasonably sure Carolyn would have told her if there had been anything encouraging about Jason's behavior. So, there was only one way to interpret it: he wasn't very devastated over their parting. He couldn't be, or Carolyn would have detected it.

Judith swallowed a lump in her throat and forced herself to accept that logic. She had no other choice.

The weather hit with a slash in the middle of the afternoon, and by early evening the countryside was awash with raging sheets of drenching rain. The river swelled in no time, rushing and rising with increasingly violent surges. There was no sign of its letting up, but Judith didn't care. Cashel was inside and all the hatches were battened down, tea was steeping and soup slowly heating on the stove. She listened absently to weather reports and travelers' adviseries on the radio as thunder crashed across the sky, driving Cashel to hide under a table. Lightning shot its ragged blazes through darkening clouds, and high winds plastered rain into the trees as an afternoon storm became a meteoric deluge.

Judith was glad to be warm and cozy inside the cabin right now, and she tried to ignore the deafening cracks of thunder by losing herself in a fantasy novel, this month's flagship publication from a book club she had joined last year.

Time got lost in the storm, and before she knew it she was halfway through the book. Since she was so involved in her reading, she was doubly startled when Cashel jumped up suddenly, almost knocking over the table he had turtled under, ran to the door and barked twice, then stood there rumbling from the bottom of his throat.

"What is it, Cash?" Judith asked, inexplicably nervous. "There's nothing out there, boy. It's only the storm. Cashel? Come lie down, boy."

But the dog refused. He continued to stand staring at the door, growling and twitching. An urgent knock at the door startled Judith breathless and sent Cashel into a reel of barks. Judith composed herself, but didn't get to the door before it opened in a splatter of rain and Jason stepped in.

Well, an echo of Jason, anyway. He was soaked to the skin, his hands wrinkled and his hair dripping in his face —a face that was a canvas of fear.

"Jason—"

"Judith, I need your help." He crossed the room to the telephone and frantically dialed. Pressing rainwater from his hair, unconcerned about the puddle of water that was forming under him, he waited for an answer on the other end and came to life when someone responded. "Did anybody find her yet? Damn. Are the police there yet? It's about time. If we find her, it'll be no thanks to them. I'll be back in half an hour." He slammed the receiver into its cradle and spun to face Judith.

"Jason, what is it?"

His voice quivered, strangely vulnerable. "Dori's missing. She wandered off when the rain started. God knows where she is by now, in this storm—" He stepped forward and grasped Judith's arms urgently. "Judith, you've got to help us. You've got to come back with me and use your clairvoyance to find her. It's her only chance. She's been gone for hours. We've done everything we could think of. Please . . . I know you detest me, but a little girl's life is hanging on your ability. Can you put up with me long enough to help?"

Wide-eyed, Judith stammered, "B-but I don't know if I can . . ." How could she tell him now, after he had driven all the way out here with her in his mind as his only hope, that her visions were gone?

"You've got to try! It's our last hope." He ran to the closet and wrenched her raincoat from it, hurried back, and swept her into it. She knew she couldn't tear away his last hope. At least she could add to the search for the child . . . or maybe there would be one last glimmer of life in her psychic mind. She doubted that, but the desperation in Jason's face crushed her heart to a pulp and left her helpless to tell him the truth.

"I can't promise anything," she said as he rushed her out to the BMW, its red paint now caked with mud. "I haven't even had a vision in weeks—"

"It's our last resort," Jason said, his breathing heavy, "or we've already lost her."

He was like a zombie during the drive to Bakerville, his hands trembling on the steering wheel. Silence dominated him most of the time, and Judith sensed he was preoccupied, running over and over in his mind the search for Dori, trying to think of a place she could be that they

171

hadn't already scoured. She didn't have to be psychic to know he was terror stricken, filled with anxiety and despair. They'd done everything humanly possible, and now he was twisted into a ball of dread, left hoping that a glimmer of chance still remained in Judith.

The weight of responsibility landed hard upon Judith's shoulders, and she too was silent, contemplating the fact that she had never had any control over her visions. How could she help find a lost child? Her heart ached for Dori, and for her parents. How helpless they must feel! How much was Jason counting on her help? Deep in her troubled heart the intense love for Jason throbbed, bringing with it a desire to assuage the fear he felt now, a desire to hold him and comfort him, to somehow be able to regain the fading clairvoyance long enough to find Dori—not only for Dori's sake, or for Carolyn or Brian, but for Jason. The love had not gone dormant, she realized; he was still foremost in her life. And he would be that much more disappointed in her when she failed to be the miracle that would save Dori's life.

She empathized with the small child, doubtless terrified and confused in a cold, wet, shapeless world, like a lost puppy—if she was still alive after all these hours. Judith felt a pinprick of guilt. How could she be thinking of herself when Dori was lost, frightened, unable to find her way into comforting arms? Judith knew that feeling all too well.

Bakerville was buzzing with search parties in the woods, down the river, down the roads. The main question: how far could an eighteen-month-old child wander? The farther away from the cottage the search progressed, the more intense and urgent it became. Dori had been gone almost half an hour before anyone noticed she was missing, and with every minute that passed the chances of finding her in the blinding downpour became worse. The wind howled and the thunder roared, drowning any tiny

172

cry or whimper that might have called someone to Dori's side if the weather had been with them.

Brian was sitting at the kitchen table, his auburn head in his hands, his crutches leaning against a chair, caked with mud. Jason went straight to him and squeezed his shoulder in useless reassurance. "Anything?"

"Nothing," Brian mumbled.

"Where's Carolyn?"

"Still out searching. They've widened the search perimeter." He covered his eyes with one quaking hand. "God, Jason, that river—if she fell in—"

"Don't think that way yet. Don't give up."

Tears welled up in Brian's blue eyes as he looked up at his brother-in-law. He was as beaten down as any man had ever been. "What are her chances? She's been gone six hours in that storm. The farther they search from our yard, the bigger the possibility that she was swept away by the current."

Judith stood watching them, unable to make a bad situation any better, she knew. She had been concentrating on Dori, trying to wrench one more clue from her mind, one more leap into the future that would give some hint of where the tiny girl could have wandered to. Abjectly she went to the window and gazed down through trees that whipped like switches in the wind, to a river that roiled as though it had come alive. The current was wild, slashing bits of wood and flotsam in its cold teeth, and Judith sadly admitted to herself that Brian was being painfully honest with himself.

"Jason," she said, trying not to disturb the somber silence that pervaded the cottage, "I'm going to go outside. Maybe the rain will help me think."

She was deliberately vague, not knowing how much Jason had told Brian about her psychic experiences, and not wanting to lead the distraught man into any false hopes.

173

Jason paused briefly, as though not knowing what to say. For a moment, Judith thought he might decide to go with her, but then he said, "Don't go far."

"I won't."

She had the river in mind. For some reason, it didn't strike her that Dori had wandered down a road; the little girl would have happened on a house or a neighbor who would have brought her home. The railroad tracks didn't seem likely . . . they weren't tough enough for an adult to walk on, much less a toddler.

Thoughtfully, Judith walked around the cottage—not an easy task in the fierce rain, with the steep hillside muddy and slippery. Then she paused. It didn't make sense to look so close to the house. This was the first area that had been searched, hours ago when Dori was first missing. The search had begun casually, because it was quite normal for Dori to wander away. It had become more and more frantic as the area of searching grew wider and wider still, and the storm grew more vicious.

All at once, Judith had an odd thought. Casually . . . the first search had been casual. Near the house. Could they have overlooked something? Could Dori still be nearby? Could she be hiding, unseen, right under their thumbs?

As unlikely as the idea seemed, Judith decided it was better than nothing. At least she wouldn't be standing around, idle, while others combed the countryside. At least it was better than waiting around for some psychic glimmer that probably would never come.

Step by difficult step, Judith began to scour the area immediately surrounding the house, looking under this and behind that, trying to remain calm and in control as the rain smacked against her raincoat and soaked her tennis shoes until it was pointless to try to keep her feet dry. After a while the hood of her raincoat had slipped off in the wind enough times that her braided hair was also sopping wet. At least it was braided and not straggling all over her face, she thought absently as she made her way down a dangerously slippery bank, toward the river that seemed to call her hungrily into its jaws. Brian's despair struck her as she clung to one tree at a time; it was incredibly dangerous even for an adult to traverse this muddy roller coaster. Dori would have had no chance.

Once she reached the riverbank, Judith paused under a fat evergreen tree that shielded her from most of the rain and scanned the riverscape. She had to hang on to a branch to keep from slipping into the river as the current rushed by mere inches away. Vision was limited as the rain drove in relentless sheets, but Judith squinted her eyes and tried to pick out any shape that might shield a child Dori's size. At first there was nothing wider than a tree, but then she noticed a lopsided rectangular structure only a few yards away—so close she had almost not noticed it at all. Changing her position to get a clearer view of it, Judith decided it was a fishing shelter of some sort, like a squat outhouse stuck a foot or two over the river, from old wood planks that were bored into the hillside. It looked as though no one had attended it in years. The roof was shabbily attached, dented in from the weather's relentless plunder, and the sides were caved in, though still holding each other up somehow. The shack was hanging out over the river precariously; the wood of the planks that supported it looked quite rotted.

"Couldn't be," Judith murmured, trying to convince herself not to try climbing out onto that awful thing. Then, "What the heck . . . things can't be any worse."

Slowly, very slowly, she edged from tree to tree along the mucky bank, slipping twice and almost becoming the river's guest for the evening, but she managed to struggle along until she could grasp the plank nearest to her. She had guessed right; the wood was rotted and bending like an old stalk of celery with each surge of the current, but she had to take the chance that it would hold out long enough for her to get a peek inside the shanty.

She climbed between the two planks and carefully put one foot at a time up onto the wood. The ground had been washed away between the planks, so she had no choice but to edge out to the shack by way of the wood rails. If only they would hold. . . .

The wind and rain beat against her as though meaning to toss her off the planks, but Judith managed to stay on and edge her way toward the shack, which had a still-intact door facing her. The wood creaked and groaned under her weight, and for one horrible moment she felt the entire structure shudder violently and shift to one side.

Judith caught her breath and froze in position.

Why hadn't she gone to get Jason before trying this? Well, she was committed. The shanty wouldn't take the strain of her climbing back, then coming out a second time.

The corner of the shanty was dipping into the river and mired on a rock against which the surging water was crashing. Hoping that rock would give the shack enough support to stay put, Judith reached for the door.

The soaked wooden panel broke free in her hand, almost throwing her off balance. The wind came by and raked the door away, taking a patch of skin from her palm along with it. She watched in horror as the door spun in the air and dove into the tumbling water of the rapids, to dance a ballet of doom until it was lost to her sight.

She repressed a fearful tremor and nudged herself closer to the shack, until she could poke her head inside and look around.

Rain was spitting in one gaping slat on the lee side of the shanty, but most of the interior was only damp from having been soaked from outside. She squinted in the darkness, but had to wait for her eyes to adjust. Anything could have been in there, from snakes to wildcats, so she

176

dared not feel around for Dori lest she disturb something else that had sought refuge from the weather.

Then, a whimper broke through the sounds of the storm battering the old shack.

Judith held her breath. Had she heard it? Or had it been merely the creaking of straining planks?

"Dori?" she called. "Answer me, honey. Are you in here?"

She heard some movement in the far corner and almost cringed away.

"I seeping, Mama," a tiny voice said.

Judith almost choked with relief. She started trembling, and was about to call out again and order Dori to come to her, but managed to keep from it. She didn't speak again until she had composed herself. She wasn't sure she could dare climb all the way into the shanty, so Dori would have to come to her. All she needed was to frighten the child into staying in her corner. "Dori, come on, honey. It's time to go home. Come on. Can you get up and come over here?"

"But I seeping."

"I know, baby, but it's not time to sleep now. Time to go home and play in the house." She extended her hand and was able to make out the dim shape of the child squatting in the corner with a fat toy hippopotamus. "Please, Dori. Come to me, honey. Hurry up."

Relief flooded her again as Dori climbed drowsily to her feet and got her balance on the slimy floor. She dropped her stuffed hippo and took precious seconds to retrieve it, but finally came toward Judith.

Judith grasped the child's coat and drew her closer, saying, "Put your arms around my neck, Dori. The ground is washed away and we have to climb a little way. Can you hang on?"

"Yes."

"What a good girl you are. Hang on tight now."

Carefully, gingerly, Judith began the slow edging backward along the planks, harder now because her balance was thrown off by Dori's weight and the awkward shape of the stuffed toy near her face. She held her breath as the shanty veered again, slipping over the rock that held it and lurching sideways, pushed by the river's current. For a moment she thought it would hold again, at least briefly, but she was wrong. A gasp cracked from her throat as the plank she was leaning on finally gave, sliding out from under her in a squish of mud and rushing water. She cried out impulsively, clamping one arm around Dori and the other over the remaining plank as she slid into waist-deep water. She felt the current dragging her legs behind her, the mud sucking her feet, providing no leverage, no bottom to push against. Dori started to cry, but she hung on to Judith like a trooper, though in her panic she let the stuffed hippo be swept away by the river.

Judith held on desperately to the remaining plank, and watched in terror as the shanty tipped completely on its side and was dragged deeper into the rapids, although the plank she was hanging on to kept it from being washed downriver. Board by board the old shanty began to separate from itself, putting more and more strain on the plank that was her lifeline as the water pulled on the structure. The plank began to bend into the current as the land it was secured into muddied and loosened. Cold water soaked her to the skin, swirling around her as though laughing at her, tasting her for its next meal, while the rain continued to sting her face, numbing her cheeks and lips, making vision dim.

Gasping, she gathered one breath and shouted, "Jason! Jason!"

Scrambling for impossible footing, she forced herself not to notice that her cries for help had been snatched up by the wind and lost only a few feet away. No one could possibly have heard.

But she kept calling. Breathing was becoming difficult as she fought the dragging current and the coldness began to penetrate her limbs, hindering her movements and sapping her strength. She would edge an inch up the plank, only to lose two inches to the yank of the river. Dori whimpered at Judith's shoulder, but luckily didn't move much. Judith wasn't sure she could have held on to a struggling child as her arms grew numb and her fingers lost their feeling.

Jason's name soon dwindled to a pathetic gasp, hardly audible to Judith herself. If only there were a way to save Dori, to put the child on shore before the raging river swept Judith's exhausted body away. If only . . .

"Judith?" A distant call was clipped short by a clap of thunder. "Judith? Where are you?"

"Ja-Jason—" Judith choked as a surge of water dragged her under momentarily. She pulled herself back up, and listened again as she tried to readjust Dori's position. The child was sputtering from the dunking, but still alive, still clinging to Judith. Judith took two deep breaths in an attempt to save enough wind for one last cry. "Jason!"

She tried to say, "Down here, in the river, by the fishing shack," but none of that got out before she was gasping again.

"We're coming! Hold on!" Jason's voice seemed far away.

"Hurry. . . ." Judith choked in a whisper. Seconds later the fishing shanty disintegrated with a series of loud creaks and was dashed downriver over the rocks. The plank Judith was clinging to began to wobble freely with each surge of the river, as though it meant to shake itself free of her. "Jason . . ." she murmured through chilled lips.

"Judith, hold on! My God . . ." Jason's form slid down the bank, swinging from one tree trunk to the next as quickly as was humanly possible. Another person was following him with equal urgency, and it turned out to be Carolyn.

"Take Dori. . . ." Judith gasped. With one numb hand she clutched Dori's clothing and pulled the child away from her, somehow managing to push her toward Jason, who tried to maintain a foothold on the muddy bank while reaching for the little girl. In a moment Dori's weight fell away from Judith's hand, and a terrible second went by before Judith realized that Jason had snatched the child and was handing her up the bank to Carolyn.

"Jason, hurry," Carolyn begged. "The plank is coming loose!"

As though on cue, the plank slid still farther from its mooring in the loosening ground and swung in a distorted arc into the rapids. Judith was swept to the end of the board, her body planing on the current, her strength being sucked out the soles of her feet.

"Hurry, Jace!" Carolyn urged.

"Judith, reach your hand out to me!" Jason called, hanging on to a pathetically thin tree branch and edging out into the river. "Please try!"

"I can't," Judith whispered, but since he didn't hear her, she gave it a try.

His fingers touched her palm, then with a single thrust he grasped her wrist and put his weight into pulling her toward him. Judith felt the river tugging greedily on her clothing; it wasn't ready to give her up. A wave crashed by and Jason lost his footing. Although he managed to keep his grip on Judith's arm, he was thrown on his side and his left knee smashed into an inconvenient rock. His face twisted in pain, but he continued to pull.

Slowly Judith's length was pushed by the current into the shoreline, and she found the strength to dig her toes into the mud and stop the drag of the water against her. Rolling into the bank, she pressed her knees downward into gritty bottom mud and was able to get one foot under her. Jason put his strength into a big yank and pulled Judith up onto the solid ground. He was able to drag himself up behind her before his bruised knee gave out.

They both lay on the sopping shore, with rain driving down and plastering their clothing to their bodies. Only Carolyn's anxious calls roused them.

"Come on," Jason said breathlessly. "Get up."

"Okay," Judith answered ridiculously, only barely remembering the gravity of the situation. She stumbled to her feet and pulled herself toward Carolyn, who extended a hand and helped her.

"How's Dori?" Judith asked. It was the only thing she could think of right now.

"Wet," Carolyn said over the sound of the rain, "but alive, thanks to you. Jason? What's wrong?"

"I hit my knee on something. I'll be up in a minute."

"I'll help you."

"No. Take Dori and Judith inside."

"Oh . . ." Carolyn muttered, worried. "Judith, are you okay? Can you carry Dori?"

"No, Carolyn, don't try it," Jason called.

"I can take her," Judith said, still panting, but beginning to think straight. She took Dori and began the slow trek up the muddy hillside, glancing back once or twice to make sure Carolyn and Jason were following. Jason was limping badly, but by the time they reached the top of the knoll and level ground in front of the house, he was putting more weight on his leg.

Numb, Judith dully said, "I'll take Dori in."

With a blank mind she entered the house.

Brian stumbled to an unsteady position on his walking cast. "Dori!"

Judith hurried to him before he tried to cross the floor on his broken leg, and he snatched the sopping child from her. "Dori, oh, baby . . . Judith . . . where'd you find her?"

181

Tears streamed down his face and merged with the rain-water that dripped everywhere.

"In the fishing shack down there," Judith murmured, still exhausted, her lips numb.

"The fishing shack . . . my God . . . all this time . . ." Brian sank down into the chair again, clutching his daughter against him, and closed his eyes. "So close. . . ."

Dazed, Judith stood dripping in the middle of the room. Odd that she had just saved a life, yet still felt so empty and worthless. She turned around on a dull thought, and wandered back toward the door. If Carolyn needed help with Jason . . .

She heard their voices even before she was outside. She opened the screen door and stepped back out into the rain—she couldn't be any wetter—and stopped dead in her tracks.

The scene before her locked her breath in her throat.

Her hands began to tremble, and not from the cold. By now the wetness had no effect on her any longer. No . . . it was something else.

Jason was standing motionless in the yard, facing Judith, but his eyes were closed as he held his sister against his chest. Carolyn's dark hair was not tied up for a change; it lay long and wet against her back as she clung to her brother in mute relief. Jason's face was lifted slightly into the rain, etched with the same peace Judith had witnessed in her vision of him and . . . but it wasn't . . . hadn't been . . . Victoria.

It was Carolyn!

Judith had been wrong . . . wrong all this time.

She slumped against the door jamb, her lips parted in abject shock. Could it be true?

Her mind scrambled to assimilate what she saw now with what she had seen in her vision. Wrong! She had been wrong!

As the truth swelled up and made itself plain to her bedraggled mind, Judith began to absorb the unfairness with which she had treated Jason. But how was she to know? Carolyn . . . his sister!

She was shaken from her amazement when Carolyn pushed herself away from Jason and wiped the tears from her mud-streaked face. "I've got to call off the search," she said shakily, "then . . . I'll make something hot to eat . . . I can't think right now . . ."

"Let's go in," Jason said, his tone laced with fatigue. He guided his sister toward the door where Judith stood as though mummified before them. Carolyn paused long enough to wrap her arms around Judith, but there were no words for what she was feeling, and she silently slipped inside the house.

Judith raised her eyes.

Jason was gazing down at her, blinking in the rain that still spattered everywhere.

"I know you don't want my company," he murmured, "but I want to thank you. For all of us."

Her throat tightened when she realized how poorly she had treated him. How could she ever expect him to forgive her now? She thought her heart would snap from the pressure of her own foolishness.

At once she caught her breath as Jason reached out and drew her against him in a surge of emotion. He caressed the nape of her neck and clutched her tight, whispering, "God, Judith, I thought I'd lost you too!"

She was caught in the wonder of his being surrounding her, quaking with fear that this might not be happening— were these Jason's arms she felt holding her as though he wanted never to let go? Was she delirious? Imagining it all?

"I don't know what I did to make you hate me," Jason was gasping huskily, "but just let me hold you a few minutes longer . . . when I saw that board slipping, I knew

183

I couldn't live without you . . . please . . . please, tell me what I did—"

"Jason!" She choked his name into his ear and wrapped her arms around him, standing on tiptoes to press her face closer against his soaked head. "Oh, my love, it wasn't you! It was my own stupidity and those damn visions! They're gone now . . . it's all over. I'm so sorry. . . ."

He drew her back to search her eyes for the final proof that she meant what she was saying. "Do you mean it?" he had to ask. "Are you sure?"

Tears burst from her eyes and she touched his wet face with both her hands. "I'm so sure," she whispered. "I'll never doubt your love again. You'll never have to prove anything to me."

His face flushed and he smiled, almost deliriously. "My beautiful Judith . . . I love you so much!" He drew her into his arms again, his lips taking possession of hers, his arms tightening around her as though he were afraid to let go.

Lost in the gentle kiss of Jason and the dribble of rain on her cheeks, Judith felt him tremble in ultimate joy against her and she knew that, though she couldn't see it, there was a destiny of love and family waiting for them both.

They stood in the rain, holding each other tight, wrapped in love's simplicity, and Judith opened her shining eyes to the sky, in time to see the clouds part and the bright moon stretch its silvery arms to light their way.

Later, when the excitement had given way to the peace of aftermath, Judith snuggled closer to Jason, turning her face into the cradle of his neck and giving in to the sensation of his arm drawing her nearer. They were resting on the bed in Jason's room, listening to a soft breeze tapping feathery fingers against the window, as though telling them they had won over the storm. Storms from the sky, storms from within themselves—all was calm now.

Jason's eyes opened from a light doze and his hand moved up her waistline to the zipper of the robe Carolyn had lent her. In a moment he had freed her breasts and was slipping the material off her shoulder.

Feeling the heat rising in his body, Judith murmured, "What will Carolyn and Brian think if we stay here all night?"

"You must be joking," Jason chuckled. "The way Carolyn practically shoved us in here together? I don't think she expects to see us until morning."

Nuzzling the soft skin under his chin, Judith said, "I can't wait to see the look on Peter's face when he hears we're getting married." She smiled warmly.

"Especially when he realizes we'll be living right there, and you'll be keeping the business." Twisting sideways on his arm, he invaded the valley between her breasts with quick swipes of his tongue.

Instantly Judith was plunged into a wilderness of sensation, riven with his fleshy explorations of her body against his, afloat in another world, a world that throbbed with hungry thrills and the possession of the man she loved. His tongue swept her throat, guided by his lips as they ran moist trails on her skin and soon claimed the gasping cavern of her mouth.

He was hers, she was his, and they celebrated their ultimate wonder with a mutuality of body and mind that was as glorious as the dawn. The enchantment was complete.

"Jason, I've never felt this way before!" Judith cried, her voice a song of joy.

"My nature goddess," he responded, holding her on top of himself and rocking back and forth with childlike rapture. "I couldn't let myself believe it at first, but I've loved you from the first moment I saw you standing at your door, wondering who in hell I was. If I ever lose you

185

. . . Judith, I don't know how I'll live." He trembled with desire and the intensity of his own words.

She drove his fears away with fondling caresses and accelerated breaths against his ear. "You'll never lose me," she whispered, "never again. I don't have to see the future to know our destiny, my love."

She felt his smile against her cheek. "You're still a sorceress," he murmured, "and I'm still under your spell."

"Forever," she breathed, and leaned into his touch.

LOOK FOR NEXT MONTH'S
CANDLELIGHT ECSTASY ROMANCES™

106 INTIMATE STRANGERS, *Denise Mathews*

107 BRAND OF PASSION, *Shirley Hart*

108 WILD ROSES, *Sheila Paulos*

109 WHERE THE RIVER BENDS, *Jo Calloway*

110 PASSION'S PRICE, *Donna Kimel Vitek*

111 STOLEN PROMISES, *Barbara Andrews*

112 SING TO ME OF LOVE. *JoAnna Brandon*

113 A LOVING ARRANGEMENT, *Diana Blayne*

When You Want A Little More Than Romance—

Try A Candlelight Ecstasy!

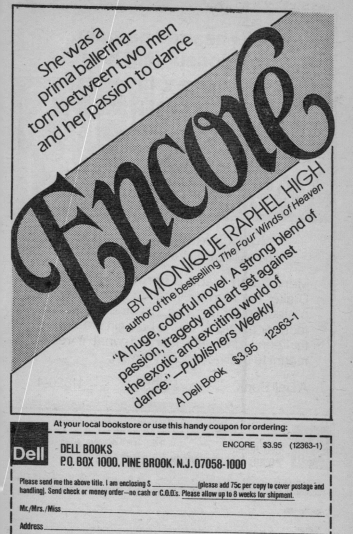

She was a prima ballerina— torn between two men and her passion to dance

Encore

BY MONIQUE RAPHEL HIGH
author of the bestselling *The Four Winds of Heaven*

"A huge, colorful novel. A strong blend of passion, tragedy and art set against the exotic and exciting world of dance." —*Publishers Weekly*

A Dell Book $3.95   12363-1

A cold-hearted bargain...
An all-consuming love...

THE TIGER'S WOMAN

by Celeste De Blasis
bestselling author of *The Proud Breed*

Mary Smith made a bargain with Jason
Drake, the man they called The Tiger: his
protection for her love, his strength to protect her secret. It was a bargain she swore
to keep...until she learned what it really
meant to be The Tiger's Woman.

A Dell Book $3.95   11820-4